While She was Dreaming

Jenny Macomber

Powerful
Potential and Purpose
PUBLISHING

www.PPP-Publishing.com

ISBN: 978-1-7361839-7-7

Any references to historical events, real people, or real places are used fictitiously. Names, characters, and places are products of the author's imagination.

Published by Powerful Potential and Purpose Publishing.
Book and cover design by Allison Chick.

Printed in the United States of America.

First printing edition 2021.

While She Was Dreaming grabs a hold of you from the first page and doesn't let go! Natalie is a compelling heroine, vulnerable yet strong. I was able to slip right inside her head as she grappled with an issue so many women are facing, not just today, but throughout history. Dreams, past lives, friendships that are soul deep, and some unfinished karmic business that threatens her soul and her sanity - I can't wait to see how her story unfolds!!!

Kari Minton, Spiritual Healer & Guide, Hypnotherapist, NLP, EFT, Reiki Master

WOW! I haven't read "recreationally" in many years, fictional books just weren't grabbing my attention or holding my interest. This book was recommended to me by a friend so I went for it and I'm so glad I did! The story really grabbed me. I felt as though I was standing unseen in the room watching Natalie's bizarre, frightening story unfold. I related very much to her, (almost a little too much!). I felt anger, anxiety, and curiosity throughout the reading. The author's skill with words and storytelling is very evident, she held my attention throughout and I'm truly excited to see more of her work. I highly recommend checking this book!

Michele Russell, Occupational Therapist

While She Was Dreaming by Jenny Macomber has really stuck with me after reading the first 5 chapters. I find myself anxiously awaiting the release of the book so I can find out how it ends.

The main character is a psychic woman dealing with vivid dreams of what could just be nightmares or memories of past lives that involved evil men. After squelching her gifts as a medium for many years she has to trust her instinct and listen to her spirit guides about strange things happening to her. The mystery is what roll do these dreams play in her present day life and have those evil characters returned to control her? The author makes it easy to care about and have empathy for the women in the dreams and gives just enough information about characters in the present day to make you start guessing who to suspect of stalking her. How will the plot twist and turn? I look forward to finding out.

Jean Dansak, Author, Healing arts professional

In *While She Was Dreaming*, Natalie, struggles to decipher the meaning of her nightmares that previously haunted her as a child but now have resurfaced. She thought they were gone. Now, using her skills as a clinical psychologist and psychic, she attempts to finally conquer the evil that has been stalking her through her past lives. The physical manifestations of events in her dreams causes her to question what is real, what is a dream, and what is imagined. Can she trust her instincts? Who is stalking her?

I look forward to reading the rest and seeing how it all unfolds.

Karlene Larsen, Physical Therapist

DEDICATION

To Paul, Morgan, Kasey and Austin with love.
Thank you for your support and gifts of time to
assist this adventure!

Chapter 1

Her wrists and ankles were each tethered to a bedpost with torn strips of old bedsheets so they wouldn't leave marks. He wanted her beautiful skin to appear pristine when she wasn't bound. She was his! No one else could have her!

Daylight was streaming a golden ray through the small castle window that rested upon her heart. She gazed around the room from her bed of imprisonment, nothing seemed to make sense. I didn't choose this life.

Shutters had been left open for fresh air. The smell of wet grass after a summer rain clung to the breeze, coupled with the powerful stench of livestock kept in the nearby barn. The sound of her only permitted companion, a dog, heard barking from a distant hall perhaps, called for her. She was alone…for now.

Hoofbeats sounded. Faint at first, they grew stronger, pounding as he pushed his horse at a gallop to carry its master home. The stable boy and house servants were chatting and scurrying around, nervously preparing for the Lord of the castle to enter. Everyone feared him and would bow their heads in his presence.

Her heart was racing! At least alone and tied up, she wasn't subjected to his cruelty. Her breathing became erratic as terror raced through a responsive body that felt a visceral reaction in her bones. Ringing in her head started as blood pumped through frantic ears. Eyes darting madly around the small stone room, she searched for a way to break free. She thrashed as hard as she could, willing the strips of binding sheet to tear and set her free. All she could think, was she needed to escape for her own life. Heavy boots were climbing and clanking along the long, narrow stone steps to the confinement of the tower room as she began to sweat with fear. Oh my God he is coming back!

The formidable wooden door creaked as Satan himself entered, smelling of sweat and horse. It was disgusting. Turning her head to the side to avoid his scrutiny, the tears dripped from her eyes knowing this could be it. Oh, dear God he is coming towards the bed, she prayed for help. Swinging his leg across the bed, he sat astride her, roughly forcing her to face him.

"Give me that beautiful face. Don't you dare turn away from the Lord of this mansion. I hope this has taught you a lesson, so next time I leave, you won't have to be bound!"

Fervently, she nodded her head in submission, head bowed, willing to do anything to keep him from torturing her, again.

"Ma Cherie, it pains me to discipline you. I expect you to behave, oui?" He sweetly cooed, pulling the gag from her mouth. Even kind words sounded like filth knowing the depth of his abusive ways.

Muscles tightening, she flinched as he bellowed for the house servant and chamber maid to tend to her and make her presentable in his sight.

Attempting to keep her gaze averted, she could not help but see the hostility in the chamber maid's eyes as they resentfully scanned her seductive body. The Maid was often jealous, but she would trade places in a second.

The house servant looked away as he cut the strips of sheet from her, doing his best not to cut her delicate skin. It tortured his heart to think he was at fault for her demise. He knew the master called him to perform this task to see what would happen were he ever again to talk to la Maitresse de Maison, or the lady of the house. The old man had felt sorry for Madame and wished nothing more than to ease her distress. Tears stung his eyes, his heart panged and his mind could not comprehend the cruelty, to see what he had inadvertently caused as he mindlessly gave her a reassuring pat on the foot. How can one person be so ruthless? he thought.

"Leave us!" the Master roared, face red and eyes bulging. "NOW!" he demanded.

"Seigneur?!" the manservant cried out in alarm, fearful of the Master's abrupt change in demeanor. He didn't want any more harm to come to the lady of the house. He feared for her life.

Drawing his rapier, a thin, light sharp-pointed sword, from its sheath, the Master plunged it into the aged servant's stomach. Falling to his knees, he clutched his chest and faded into unconsciousness. Ripping the blade from his torso, withdrawing the weapon, he then held it against her throat, bloodying her gown and silencing her screams. Sadistic as always, he roared. "Did you enjoy his touch?!" he seethed with deranged notion.

"You are mad! He is simply a sweet old man!" screaming hysterically, she caught the element of surprise as she grabbed the hilt of the sword with her freed hand. Struggling and bantering with the sword, it caught him on the cheek, causing blood to flow from the wound. His mind past the brink of insanity, he gained control of the weapon. Turning it on her, a warlike battle cry echoed through the castle as he swung. It was as if he enjoyed this sort of sick play.

"STOP!" she bellowed.

Natalie woke herself with a stifled scream still hanging in her throat, drenched in sweat and gasping for air. Heart pounding so fiercely it felt as though it would explode, Natalie scanned her usually soft, inviting bed to see if there were any signs that may clue her into what had just happened. She attempted to straighten the strewn sheets, which looked more as if they had been torn from their resting place and used to fight off an imaginary force. A cool sensation from the air conditioning snapped Natalie back to reality as she tried to banish vivid images from her mind. The frigid air met with damp hair. Cuddled in her soft comfy pajamas, it sent tingles up her spine, making her shiver. It was so real she could physically feel its effects. She clutched at her chest where the emotional trauma hung as if the scene had actually happened. Natalie didn't see herself in the dream, but sensed she was the prisoner. Why was she dreaming of herself in a medieval castle in France?

Nightmares hadn't occurred since childhood

and vague recollections of her terrifying visions brought Natalie back to when she was an ashamed little girl.

"People are coming to get me!" Natalie cried to her mother upon awakening from a nightmare. At first, little Natalie was indulged. When it became apparent she had the ability to see Spirits and to just know things, Natalie's father demanded she be punished for being possessed by the devil. Kneeling at the foot of her bed, hands in prayer position every night, she begged forgiveness for talking to evil spirits. A private counseling session with the church pastor demeaned and shamed little Natalie for her exaggerated imagination. They certainly dismissed unusual abilities as gifts growing up, and called them curses. Having no one to guide her, these abilities went undeveloped and unacknowledged. Natalie learned not to give the energies in her childhood dreams any attention. As she ignored them, they eventually faded. However, as an adult, they were back with a vengeance and Natalie knew if she didn't figure out why, she might not survive. But why now?

She desired to please her father and be perceived as an obedient daughter. Natalie conformed to her parent's wishes. Forcibly silenced, she shared her innate perceptions of visitors in nightmares and spirits who randomly appeared, to her best friend, Lisa and her brother Andrew.

Fear of being ostracized as a freak and of word getting back to her parents within their small community kept Natalie stifled. Her lone childhood friend, Lisa, helped Natalie feel as though she was special, with a secret superpower. "No one can learn of your gift," she whispered to her friend. We shall play with it and one day I imagine it will come in handy." In their childhood innocence that is exactly what they would do. Eventually they both developed a deep connection few would understand.

As an educated adult pursuing her own degree in psychology, Natalie later understood her mother didn't intend to make her feel bad. She was merely afraid for her little girl and didn't have the skillset or knowledge to help her child. As a dutiful wife, she dared not betray rules her husband enforced either. Natalie's father was a stern man who liked to preach about being a God-fearing servant while behaving as he pleased. He would be in control of how his family behaved. Churches in the small towns of Western North Carolina put the fear of the wrath of God into their parishioners, which is what Natalie's parents reacted to. There was plenty of love to be had for those who "obeyed" and plenty of hatred for those who didn't follow the strict doctrine that was doled out like propaganda. As children, Natalie and her younger brother, Andrew, despised Sunday school, dreaded annual vacation bible school and had a mutual, unspoken disbelief of organized religion. They both felt something within nature that gave them peace and lessons, although neither sibling could articulate their perceptions; they just knew. Questions went unspoken between them and why their mother's Native American heritage was discarded. It would take many years to find their own spiritual path that resonated with them as adults. With the help of a Spiritual Healer, Ben, Natalie was understanding herself, able to define her beliefs, and validate her *superpowers*. Volunteering on the Cherokee reservation during the clinical years of obtaining a degree had led her to meet Ben, who helped unleash the world that Natalie had repressed all her life.

A jolt of energy filled her with goose bumps shaking Natalie from her reverie. It was crazy how one memory could take her far back to so many recollections. Maybe a shower would free her thoughts. She had a hectic day to focus on.

Natalie slid her toned body from the wreckage of the bed and stumbled to the bathroom mirror. She closely examined a perfectly oval, tanned face, looking for signs of trauma from what felt more real than any dream. She couldn't help but notice faint red markings around her wrists. Alarmed, she examined them, noting they didn't hurt. Have I been mindlessly rubbing my wrists?" She thought incredulously. An eerie sensation crept into her mind as she thought to look down at her ankles. Natalie shrieked at the sight of the same red marks at the base of her legs. "Oh my God! What the hell is going on?"

Reliving this nightmare with flashes of images, caused her stomach to heave. *You were tied to a bed*, an inner voice reminded her. Firmly placing her hands on the cold counter, she steadied herself as a reeling headache threatened her stability. How can I possibly have marks on my body from a nightmare? Wide, brilliant blue eyes met her own gaze in the mirror; eyes full of disbelief. Shadows of gray and puffiness beneath them told of restless nights and other recent nightmares. Natalie's long, dark hair swung from side to side as she shook her head, not prepared to analyze what was happening. I can't do this right now, she argued with herself, reaching into the shower for the spicket.

Hot water trickled down her back, calming tense muscles as Natalie washed away the remnants of the nightmare. She imagined the water to be nurturing and purifying, swirling the fear down the drain, believed by her Native American ancestors. Taking a deep breath in, down to her abdomen, she paused. Softly separating her lips, she slowly released her breath, further calming mind and body. This is good, she thought.

Thank you, God, for a hot shower, she thought

Geez, I feel like a hypocrite for calling you God since I don't believe in organized religion, but it's the name I always revert to without thinking. I've tried Great Spirit, and that feels more appropriate, but somehow God comes to mind first. Maybe it's because conditioning began at such a young age, God is the word ingrained in my mind. Natalie pondered her word choices, momentarily distracting herself.

Wrapped in a large towel and feeling more in control, she examined herself again in the mirror. The warm water had helped blood circulate, and she was more satisfied with her appearance. Electric eyes still reflected the horror she couldn't shake of the nightmare and its lingering effects. Who am I looking at, she pondered? Knowing her dark hair and illuminated eyes always drew attention, she wished it wouldn't be ridiculous to wear sunglasses inside at work. However, she surely didn't want her clients thinking someone punched her in the face. She chuckled at the thought and got ready.

A giant cup of coffee with scrambled eggs and avocado gave her the time to wander back to the nightmares and why they were happening. Even though she consciously knew better as an adult and especially as a Clinical Psychologist, the little girl who they made feel evil couldn't shake the guilt. Natalie contemplated... maybe the recent, returned nightmares were punishment for discounting her gifts. *If I had just acknowledged them, would they be tormenting me now? Well, that sounds like a Sunday morning service.* She laughed at herself. But evil spirits really do exist, so what if they've gained access to my unconscious mind because I didn't learn how to protect myself? Considering that this time there were physical marks left, what if there's an entity tormenting me? She needed a private session with Ben. It would have to wait until she visited the Reservation on Saturday. It didn't seem too far away...

Reveling the view from the window of her third story apartment, the blue ridge mountains beckoned. She loved how it felt to walk through the woods, especially if there was a creek or a river to follow. Something about the hypnotic sound of the water contrasted against the green of the trees captivated her senses. Taking in the beauty of dawn breaking, an eerie sensation washed over her. *You're mine,* she heard. It wasn't really a voice, but words that made themselves known in her mind. Jumping away from the window, Natalie ran fingers through her hair, laced them behind her head and squeezed her arms and elbows tightly, as if to keep her head from exploding. "Oh, hell no!" she screamed out loud. "Night time is bad enough! I won't lose my mind during the day too!"

Resolved to reconnect with her neglected abilities, Natalie chose the large overstuffed chair in the small living room to sit in. The nightmare had gotten her up early, so she had time before her first patient. She sunk into soft fabric, which enfolded around her, making Natalie feel as though she were in a cocoon. Breathing deeply once again, Natalie tried to clear her mind. Chilling words reverberated through her mind as the determination to gain control of herself set in. First, she forgot to keep breathing. *For something that is vital to life, how can I possibly forget to breathe?* She sarcastically asked herself. *Maybe if I ask my ancestors to guide me, that will help?* She tried to clear her mind again and silently asked for guidance. Nothing. Did I put the clothes in the dryer yesterday? Oh, good grief! Why is meditating so hard?! Natalie jumped out of the chair and checked the washer; nope, wet clothes in there. Well, it's a good thing I meditated for two minutes! My guides successfully told me to put the clothes in the dryer, she joked to herself. Attempting to meditate had worked in an odd sort of way. Humor had replaced fear, and that would have to do for now. Learning to discipline her mind was going to take time and practice even though she had *gifts.* Why can't they just get better on their own? Why do I have to *develop* them? Aggravated, she poured a thermos of coffee to take to work. She was going to need the extra caffeine today.

Chapter 2

Natalie found satisfaction in her job as a Clinical Psychotherapist, although today her eyes were tired and her mind distracted. Trauma and Post Traumatic Stress Syndrome were her specialty, which helped her process her own disturbing nightmares. *Maybe I should branch out and include traumatic dream interpretation in my treatment,* she jokingly mused to herself. Natalie couldn't help but wonder if maybe she needed to do a better job of shielding herself from her patients' energy or emotional devastation. *Could this be the cause of having nightmares?* She was pretty good at leaving work behind and not ruminating over her patient's challenges. Today, however, she was ruminating over traumas; her own, and it was affecting her job performance. *What will I do about this? Stay focused in the present moment,* she heard in her head.

Glancing down at her wrists throughout the day, curious, she inspected the red marks, holding her breath until assured they had faded. Her mind reverted to the vivid nightmare as her eyes glassed over, staring ahead, but seeing nothing. Patients could tell she was distracted, which filled her with guilt. Questions were repeated and one of her client's suggested she take the day off. The therapist needs therapy; she wanted to tell them. A full schedule of patients and charting notes made the day feel endless. Endlessly writing and not really paying attention to anything important, a sense of relief washed over her as she finished up with the last patient. Getting outside was going to feel so good, she anticipated, as she left the office.

Natalie breathed in the sweet scent of mountain air walking from her office at Mission Hospital to her nearby apartment, clearing the thoughts and emotions which had plagued her all day. It was within Biltmore Park Town Square, which was the newest and most popular destination to live and play in Asheville, NC. She felt spoiled by having shops, restaurants, entertainment, the hospital, and workout options right there in the planned community. REI was having a sale, so she popped in to see if there were any items she couldn't live without before going home. I love how safe and intimate it feels to live here, she observed. I'm sheltered from the rest of the city, she felt. Natalie enjoyed having a fun city to explore, but she also needed plenty of places for outdoor adventures. The proximity of the Blue Ridge Parkway provided plenty of options especially when the rhododendron bloomed or the fall colors draped along the highway and the nearby trails. If cooking dinner was unappealing, she could pop into any restaurant down in the Town Square. Her mind expected a much needed evening run as she unlocked the door.

The heels were the first thing to come off, stripping as soon as the door closed behind her. She stretched her neck from side to side, letting her head roll around, loosening the stored tension. Breathing in and then letting out a forced breath of air, she willed anxiety from her body just like yoga taught her. Ripping off her confining work clothes she placed them responsibly in the hamper and returned her shoes to their place in the closet. A tidy home gave her mind fewer things to stress about. Donning comfortable leggings, a t-shirt, and her favorite Nike's, Natalie felt more like herself and was ready for a run.

Once outside in the cool, slightly humid evening air, she lightly jogged down a favorite trail. Taking in the beauty of the wooded path with a deep sigh, her tension from the unnerving nightmare coupled with the highly charged emotions of patients flowed out of her body. Exercise seemed to be the best kind of stress relief, since meditating made her fidgety. Her overactive mind wandered and got frustrated with having to sit still, was made clear that morning. Movement helped Natalie clear her thoughts and connect to herself, especially if it was outside. She picked up the jogging pace, heading into a second mile. Her silky dark hair swishing in a ponytail, trees embraced her as the sky turned light pink with the setting sun. Her soul felt at home and communed with nature. She could always feel the forces of nature. Oddly, though, something didn't feel right in her gut. I've got to figure this out and deal with it, she counseled herself as a boisterous growl came from her stomach. Thank goodness it was Monday, and she had a standing restaurant order waiting to be picked up when she finished running! A gentle breeze kissed her cheek, which felt like it came from *someone* who loved her.

P.F. Chang's, a restaurant in the Town Square, was her favorite. Every Monday, and sometimes other days as well, an order of Mongolian Beef was waiting for pickup at 6:30. Natalie stopped by after her much needed stress reducing run, waved hello to the staff who knew her, and headed up to her apartment.

Natalie settled into the corner of a plush cream colored couch, sinking into the fluffy pillows after exchanging running shoes for cozy slippers. Sighing with exhaustion, she pulled her legs up on the couch beside her, tucking chilled feet under a throw blanket made for her.

She delicately balanced her dinner plate on top of another pillow, ready to devour the tempting smells of Mongolian Beef that teased her taste buds. A glass of luscious red blend had already been halfway consumed before being carefully placed on a side table. Natalie knew a cream couch and red wine were probably not the safest choices to combine, but like the magnet on her refrigerator read, *knowing better has never stopped me.*

Almost through with dinner, the sound of a chime indicated a text was waiting to be read. Natalie winced and groaned. *No, go away!* Ignoring the phone, she finished dinner and the wine, determined to unwind and get some rest. Two more chimes sounded as a persistent friend continued to send messages. Grudgingly, Natalie picked up the phone and checked. Lisa, her best friend from childhood, was down at the Monk's Flask brewery. Joining her were a few other members of their high school tribe that remained close knit throughout the years. The fun-loving gang of friends were like brothers and sisters to each other. They were terrible at planning anything, so spontaneously they showed up and texted each other to join in random fun.

"I just finished dinner and am turning in early. No sleep last night," Natalie texted back.

"One drink!" Lisa pleaded. "We're right here in

the Square. It's not like you have to drive anywhere! Walk down for a nightcap! I'll buy!"

"I went for a run. I need a shower!" Natalie tried to argue.

"It's just us. Who cares?" Lisa was not giving up.

"Ok fine," Natalie reluctantly surrendered. She adored her surrogate siblings. A good brushing through long, almost black hair improved the appearance enough to satisfy her. Quickly applying a precautionary bit of deodorant and throwing on a light jacket, Natalie took the stairs to get in a few more steps.

"There she is!" the group of friends called out from a table inside the brewery as she entered.

"I can't stay long. I've got patients first thing in the morning."

"We're your patients! God knows we all need help!" one of them joked, eliciting a round of laughter and high-fives.

"Lisa, do you want to split a glass of wine with me? I've already had some with dinner. I don't need another whole glass."

"Oh, good grief, Nat!" Lisa rolled her eyes. "It's a restaurant pour, which hardly counts! Besides, I already ordered for you."

Natalie was the mother of the group, always attempting to be the voice of practicality, but it often fell on deaf ears. She allowed herself to let loose more than usual with them, knowing they had her back and would lay down their lives for her. Laughing at Lisa, she held her glass up to cheer with the rest of the boisterous gang.

"I want you to meet someone!" Lisa seemed coy. Her sea-green eyes cut sideways to indicate she was referring to a devastatingly handsome guy standing at the end of the table, talking to some of their other friends.

Sharp icicles stabbed through Natalie's body, replacing the warm sensation of the wine with jolting sensations of shock. Her body's response caught Natalie off guard as she inspected him from a distance. *What was that?*

"That is Jared," Lisa whispered... "Whaddya think?" she girlishly giggled.

Trying to hide her strange feelings, Natalie took a swallow of wine. Thank goodness Lisa got her own glass! "Who is he? I assume this is a romantic interest?"

"Mayyyyybe,"

"Well, he certainly is tall, dark and handsome." A cliché was the best Natalie could come up with. Was she attracted to him? Definitely. But there was something else that unnerved her. And he was her best friend's latest romantic interest. Dammit, she should have stayed on the couch! This day started off horribly and now it's going to end the same way. The song "I should probably go to bed" by Dan and Shay started singing in her mind.

"Thanks for that," she wryly snipped at the Universe. "You're so funny," she added, irritated that it was accurate.

Adrenaline streaming through her body, Natalie did her best to take in focused deep breaths without being obvious that she was fighting for self-control. A slight tremor in her hand made the wine glass shake. Noticing the marks on her wrists once again, she took another sip.

"Are you okay?" Concerned, Lisa put a hand on Natalie's shoulder to comfort her.

"Geez, I'm sorry I pressured you to come down! We can leave and talk in private instead."

"No, no, I'm good! Really! Just a long day with no sleep. It's catching up with me."

"Okay, I get the long day, but why no sleep?"

Lisa knew her better than anyone. She and Natalie were inseparable growing up. They were the sister neither had. Lisa knew all about the childhood nightmares, unusual gifts, and spirits and she knew the nightmares had returned.

Not wanting to worry her, Natalie sidestepped the question and changed the subject. "So, tell me about Jared!"

Knowing damn well what her best friend was doing, Lisa let it go–for now. "He came into the gallery a couple of weeks ago just looking around. We talked, of course, exchanged numbers, and had lunch twice. Nothing serious! Just having fun!"

"Does he know you're the queen of just having fun?" Natalie joked.

"We haven't had a serious enough conversation to go there yet. I told him about you and our crazy gang and he wanted to meet you all, so here we are!" Lisa threw her hands up in the air as if presenting herself on stage.

Natalie wrinkled her nose and smiled at her adorable friend. Lisa's strawberry blonde hair and green eyes made her look more as if she belonged on a beach in California. The two of them couldn't be more opposite in appearance if they tried. The only wrinkle in their friendship was Lisa's jealousy over Natalie's boyfriends.

"Did he at least buy a painting or something, or was he just checking you out?"

"Oh, he really was there looking for a painting! I sold him one of my mysterious, dark masterpieces. Guys like that kind of stuff, you know. Now I'll have to paint something to accompany it so he can have a collection." Lisa gave a wink, as if there were ulterior motives.

There's no way to avoid meeting Jared, so I might as well take advantage of the liquid courage and humor Lisa, she lamented, finishing the glass of wine with an unladylike gulp. Natalie couldn't identify what she felt that made her so uneasy, but she sure as hell would not run from it, so she followed Lisa through the crowd.

A strong sense of déjà vu washed over her as Jared's dark eyes turned and bored into her soul. Tousled dark, slightly wavy hair made Natalie want to entwine her fingers in it. A sultry smile from full lips made her unconsciously lick her own. The surrounding room disappeared as Jared and Natalie's energies created their own time warp. Natalie's breath was literally taken away as weakness caused her knees to give way. Jared caught her with strong, sculpted arms, as the stunning sensation of his touch only made matters worse. A vaguely familiar ringing started in her ears as she gasped for air. Are my ears ringing because I'm faint or because my guides are trying to convey a message? She wondered. I feel like I'm in a dream; she thought, while fighting to remain conscious.

Concerned and curious eyes turned to see what was happening. Placed precariously on a barstool, Natalie managed an embarrassed smile as a glass of water was placed in front of her. Using it as a distraction, she focused her attention on the glass, averting her eyes, but it was no use. Jared and Lisa were hovering around her just in case she fell off the stool. Natalie dragged her gaze to Jared, hoping she wouldn't make an idiot of herself again. His eyes sparked a familiarity in her subconscious.

"Sorry about that! Thanks for catching me!" she tried to make light of the incident, wondering if he experienced any of the extreme sensations she had. "I probably had one too many glasses of wine after a sleepless night. I felt a little woozy."

"My pleasure, entirely," a deep, smooth voice assured, making her insides flip as he stood too close, emanating a powerful sexual energy towards Natalie.

Apparently, he felt the same sensations. Natalie worried to herself as the look on Lisa's face bordered on jealousy. *Whoa that's intense.*

"I'm used to reactions like that. Women fall at my feet. It's a curse and a gift that has followed me through lifetimes," Jared crooned, trying to make his words seem like a joke, but his energy felt otherwise. Pulling Lisa close to him with his hand wrapped possessively around her waist, Jared ran his free hand up Natalie's back seductively.

"Was the wine you were drinking Ménage à Trois?

That's always been a favorite of mine," he insinuated as his fingers tugged at her long hair, gently jerking her neck backwards.

Natalie was speechless by his audacity but also triggered to feel anger and fear when he pulled her hair. Lisa thankfully interrupted what was sure to be a catastrophe if Jared kept talking.

"Okay. I let it go earlier. Now you need to talk to me!" Lisa used Natalie's swooning spell to change the subject and insert herself in between Jared and Natalie. "I'm walking you back to your apartment. Jared can help me if you're not stable enough." She narrowed her eyes at him as if to indicate he should decline her polite offer.

"NO!" Natalie didn't mean to scream, but wasn't about to have him accompany her anywhere. It was bad enough he knew where she lived. She questioned her attraction to her best friend's boy toy or if the strange familiarities scared her. Jared would love to escort both her and Lisa to the bedroom for a threesome she sensed, but out of respect for Lisa, Natalie didn't act on her impulse to slap him across the face. *Who the hell is this guy and why does he seem familiar?* Nothing was making sense about him, and she just wanted to get some space to clear her head.

"I'm sorry… I mean, no thank you, I'm okay to

walk home." Natalie put her hand up to indicate there would be no arguing about it. "Like I said earlier, I just really need to go to bed." The song 'I Should Probably Go to Bed' started playing in her head again. Ugh, they're always right. One of these days I'll listen when I'm given messages, she ruefully thought. One thing was sure; Natalie never lost her sense of humor, especially if directed at herself!

"I'm at least walking you." Lisa had a stern look on her face that meant she wasn't giving in.

"Have you guys met before?" Lisa almost demanded to know. There was a harshness in her voice as they made their way to the apartment. Natalie was thinking about how she should answer the question.

"Not that I know of," Natalie tried to answer as vaguely as she could without revealing the combustive emotions exchanged between herself and Jared. "I hope he's just someone for you to have fun with; I wouldn't trust him any further than I can throw him."

The comment seemed to disarm Lisa somewhat as she relaxed.

"I'm not looking for a husband," Lisa sarcastically smiled.

"Yeah, but you don't need a cheater or an STD,

either!" Natalie returned the smile with some attitude alongside.

"Yes, mother!" Lisa rolled her eyes.

Hugging, they parted ways after Lisa was satisfied Natalie would be okay by herself.

The sanctuary of her apartment had never felt so good. Natalie could put Lisa off quickly, since Jared was waiting for her in the bar downstairs. A soft rubbing against her shins showed that her cat, Sage, wanted some attention. Kneading her arm and purring loudly, Sage drained the anxiety from Natalie as she collapsed into the overstuffed chair along with her overstuffed cat. Stroking Sage's luxurious, long, soft white fur brought Natalie's mind back down to Earth. Sage looked more exotic and elegant than her name implied, but Natalie wanted her name to be more representative of her own life as opposed to the cat's. She had learned to use sage from the Indians on the reservation, where she had also gotten the kitten. It was *sacred* to them and she appreciated the sanctity of the plant as it represented her ancestral culture. Natalie would use a bundle of dried sage wrapped in twine she obtained from the Cherokee Reservation. When she volunteered there, the shaman taught her how to use it for cleansing energies and tonight was the perfect night for a cleanse. This involved lighting the end of the wound bundle to where it smoked and then letting the smoke curl into all the corners of her apartment, while repeating a chant. It appeared a thorough saging was in order, but not tonight even though she knew she should definitely apply this ceremony. She was physically and mentally drained.

Reluctantly, she let her mind replay the evening. It perplexed Natalie why she had such a visceral reaction to Jared and why the scar on his face reminded of her someone, somewhere. I know I would remember meeting someone who affected me like that! Even if I hadn't, I would remember someone with this intense chemistry who seems to think we should have sex! *You can NOT feel this attraction to your best friend's crush!* She firmly told herself. Ugh, hopefully Lisa will tire of him sooner than later and this won't be an issue. Fat chance, the voice in her head countered. She squirmed at the uncomfortable thoughts as Sage jumped off her lap.

Looking out the window again at the sapphire night sky, Natalie vaguely remembered the eerie feeling she had just that morning as the sun was rising. Had it been a premonition about tonight? *No, that wouldn't make sense.* The words *you're mine* didn't fit with the events in the bar. Maybe I need a psychologist myself, she only half way joked. I'd rather see Ben first and get his perspective on it. The thought of consulting with the Spiritual Healer who had become a friend and a father figure took some of the anxiety away. Guidance from Spirit soothed her mind and heart. Natalie was going to have to learn to trust her gifts and intuition much more and do a better job.

"I have GOT to get rest tonight," she informed Sage, who responded with a sweet little meow as she crawled into bed. "I took an anxiety pill to help, don't tell anyone." Sage responded by purring loudly and snuggling up close. Natalie's mind granted her request... until the early morning hours when another nightmare stole the tranquility of sleep.

Chapter 3

Sofia stood shaking violently beside Hatar at the altar as she dutifully married a man twice her age. Knowing nothing of being a wife, she did not wish to become one at thirteen, despite tradition in Malaysia that allowed and even encouraged child brides.

Despair filled her body as she anticipated acts he would force her to endure.

Sensing her terror, it filled Hatar with sadistic excitement as his primal urge to dominate her consumed him. "I thought taking you as my bride would dull all enjoyment, but your fear makes this an even more tantalizing game," he cruelly whispered in her ear so the Imam could not hear, pulling her closer by her long hair.

A cold sweat broke out across Sofia's lovely face, threatening to ruin the makeup intended to match the formality of the embroidered ceremonial gown borrowed for the occasion. Without warning, she vomited on the floor at their feet, soiling their shoes, unable to endure Hatar's words.

Outside of the small mosque, the Imam, the ones committed to their faith and pray for others, found and attempted to comfort the distraught girl, patting her arm as she sought fresh air. "You are always welcome to find sanctuary here, my child. I pray Allah will protect you and bring happiness."

Sofia looked into the tender eyes of Amir, who had always been the Imam in the village, guiding the children in the teachings of Islam. Sofia had been a troublesome student, challenging the unfairness of the practice exercised towards females. Amir took a liking to her intelligence and enjoyed their conversations. He had become a father figure to her after the passing of her own father years ago.

Amir's large white dog appeared at the sound of Sofia's voice. She had been a source of comfort to Sofia whenever she came to the Imam for lessons or to help with chores at the mosque. Jumping up and placing her dusty paws on the beautiful wedding gown, the dog licked Sofia's face, further eroding her appearance.

"Hatar is a demon who will torture me!" she cried.

Intuitively, she knew. Her tears left colored streaks of the dense cosmetics dripping on her gown mixed with the dog's saliva as she lovingly returned its affection.

"You are understandably fearful of what you do not know. Rinse your mouth with some water."

"No! When he sticks his serpent tongue in my mouth, he will taste vomit!"

Amir admired Sofia's fortitude, but could not bring himself to smile this time, sympathetic to her despair. Sofia's mother, Farah, appeared, chastising her daughter for vomiting and running out. Scanning Sofia's youthful body, her eyes filled with repugnance, she chastised Sofia and Amir. "Stop placating her drama! Both of you return and spare us further embarrassment!"

"She is jealous," Sofia whispered as Amir performed a blessing over her. "I have seen Hatar and my mother together. He covets me, which makes her envious. There are many things I do not believe about Allah, but I do not believe he smiles down upon a mother who is jealous of her own child." Sophia cast her eyes upon a beautiful, ancient amulet hanging from Amir's neck. It intrigued her. She wanted to know more, but her mother interfered.

Eyes narrowed, Farah hissed at her child, "What lies do you spread?!"

"It is your fault I must marry this vile man!"

Sofia's head lurched to the side as the palm of Farah's hand met with a crack against her daughter's face. Amir grabbed Farah by her shoulders and firmly pushed her out of the way of his growling dog as it snapped, safeguarding its anguished young friend. The amulet glowed. How odd, Sophia thought.

"GO," he bellowed, pointing inside with anger flashing in his eyes.

With Farah back inside, the tenderness in Amir's eyes returned as he patted her hand again and asked, "Who shall repair your paint?"

Sophia managed a smile. "It's called makeup and no one shall repair it! I shall marry a monster looking like a monster, myself!" She defiantly stuck her chin up and put an arm out for Amir to escort her inside. They had a fond connection that felt like it had been there for a thousand years.

At the altar once again, dressed in formal wedding attire, Sofia and Hatar completed the required ceremony for marriage. Sofia defiantly focused her gaze upon her envious mother, not understanding why she would feel desire for the devil. The congregation of villagers dutifully waited for the union. Several of the local women sought counsel with Sofia for a unique gift of insight she displayed.

They bowed in prayer, knowing she would not be accepted by Hatar or his followers.

Whispers about Sofia's appearance were heard as the couple made their way out of the mosque. Although a young woman, her beauty was undeniable. Hatar's face was taut with ire, his blood boiling at the scene she had made. Sofia knew her satisfaction would be short lived, but she would cling to the only measure of control she could find.

His hut was just as one would expect a man's dwelling to be, sparse and filthy. Just like him, Sophia thought. Wishing she had courage, nerves got the better of her as she accepted there was no escape. This was her life. He was her husband, and she had to obey him. Defiance meant he could do anything he wished to her without punishment. The thought crossed her young mind. Do I want to live or die? I honestly don't know. Before having time to complete the thought, Sofia landed on the floor, knocked out by an angry blow to the jaw from Hatar. Searing pain and helplessness were her last memories as she drifted into another world.

Hours later, Sofia awoke to an intoxicated husband, and her body half clothed. The stench of his breath alerted her to his repugnant presence as she stiffened in alarm, shoulders and arms held tight while her legs felt like wet rice noodles. A slight scream escaped her as Hatar's voice alone struck terror within her heart. He had violated his own wife while being unconscious, noticing drips of blood on her white gown.

"You are never to speak to the Imam again," he slurred.

"He is like a father to me and helps me abide by the wishes of Allah!" she panicked, as the thought of never speaking to Amir paralyzed her thoughts.

"He lusts for you, as do all men in the village! You are to speak to only me! I made you my wife to keep you from them! You belong to me! No man will want you now, for I have entered your chamber and marked you, forever. You WILL conform to my demands!"

"I am your wife, but I belong only to myself!" Sofia foolishly argued. He could not even respect his wife's decision for not wanting to have sex when she menstruates. How will he respect any of my wishes? "He won't," she heard a voice speak to her.

Enraged, Hatar grabbed a machete used for clearing vegetation. He raised it and lunged towards Sofia, losing his balance and falling to the floor. Inebriated, he lost consciousness, and the weapon sliced his face as it clanged to the ground beside him. Sofia cautiously approached, checking if he was alive. He was breathing normally but passed out from excess drink. Her mind raced as she contemplated the blood streaming from the gash on his cheek.

"He will awake and accuse me of this wound! There will be a scar!" she frantically assessed. Believing he would kill her upon waking, Sofia resolved to do the only thing she knew of. She set out on foot as the twilight of day painted the sky with brilliant pinks and blues. Trees swayed in the gentle breezes while birds sang upon arising. Feeling numb in her heart, Sofia made her way to a favorite cliff overlooking the mighty sea. As she lifted her eyes to the heavens, she said a prayer; "Please look after Amir and let him know when I am safe." Without hesitation, she jumped.

Chapter 4

Natalie woke herself from yet another nightmare, bolting upright in bed, screaming with the sensation that she had been falling. "Where am I?"

Wild eyes scanned the room as adrenaline rushed through her body, telling her to fly. A confusing sense of being in two places at one time disoriented her frantic mind. She reached out with her hands, attempting to either steady herself or catch her plunge.

A disgruntled look from Sage, sprawled out against the other pillow, brought instant grounding and relief. Clutching her chest, Natalie fought to get her breathing and heart rate under control. With details of the nightmare still fresh in her mind, she wondered, did I jump off a cliff? Realizing, without consciously thinking, that the woman in the nightmare was, again, herself. Confusion caused

Natalie to scrunch her forehead as she noted the increased detail of the nightmare and familiarity of the characters besides herself. "I must write this down". Head cocked to the side in contemplation, she reflected, there are similarities happening in the themes of these nightmares! I'm helpless because of an abusive husband, there's a caring father-like figure, and a jealous woman, she diligently scribbled across a piece of paper. Nightmares have a common thread. Could these be a premonition or past life memory? Another thought burst through her mind. They don't leave marks, either. A quick assessment of her body revealed no broken bones from a fall, but an aching jaw. Shaking her head, Natalie wondered, *what the hell is happening?!*

Flopping back down and burying herself in the pillow's softness, she stretched her arm out to stroke Sage's fur. The exotic-looking feline responded to Natalie with loud purring, while rolling over to display her plump belly as she stretched. Tapping into Sage's comforting energy, Natalie kept her mind focused on the vibration of the purring and the sensation of soft fur beneath her hand. She drifted off to a much-needed sleep and missed an early staff meeting.

Threatening clouds obscured the sun as Natalie walked from her apartment to her office at the nearby hospital. *I could really use some sunshine to lift this fog out of my head,* she observed. A tingle ran up her back as she sensed someone was watching. Not trusting her instincts after two nightmares and a strange encounter the night before, she picked up the pace and got to the hospital, without the custom of taking in the trees and scenery she felt a part of. There was no sign of her first patient, Mr. Edward Bowden. "Call me Ed," he would nervously chide. Natalie made it a strict policy to keep a professional relationship with her patients. It would be too easy to cross the line into friendship and take on their problems as friends do. Mr. Bowden took care of his elderly, overbearing mother. A fairly new patient, Natalie was only uncovering the damage to his self-confidence that had resulted from his domineering parents. He had never married and had no siblings, so was the only option for his mother's care, as she refused a nursing home. Feeling sorry for the sweet, obedient man, Natalie perused their session notes to decide what path to take in his treatment. Something told Natalie his mother had a secret, but he never spoke about it.

Sensing a presence, Natalie jumped at seeing Mr. Bowden standing in the doorway to her office.

"I'm so sorry! I didn't mean to scare you!"

"Oh, goodness! Nothing to be sorry about," she

smiled, trying to conceal her jumpy nerves. "Please come in and make yourself comfortable."

"I brought you a latte from Starbucks. I stopped in to get myself something and thought you might need a little morning pick-me-up. It's made with almond milk since you stay looking so fit."

Natalie almost froze as electric sensations threatened to paralyze her extremities. Am I getting hit on or am I just being paranoid after the run-in with Jared, she couldn't help but wonder? And how does he know I take almond milk? I'm having my own PTSD, she quickly deduced. Mr. Bowden is a people pleaser and we've got to work on that for him. Instantly regaining her composure after her reassuring assessment, Natalie knew which topic to address in the day's session. First, a deep cleansing breath.

In some ways, Natalie could relate to Mr. Bowden's inability to escape the imperious expectations of his parents, even though his father was deceased. It was natural for a child to want to please their parents. But at some point, she felt, you've got to grow into a sense of who you are and develop your own values; a lack of self-confidence prevents people from setting healthy boundaries. Natalie knew this feeling all too well.

Her own parents were afraid of Natalie's gifts being

discovered by anyone outside of the family for fear they would ostracize her. As an adult, she could look back and understand and forgive them. However, it took years of healing and forgiveness. It had damaged her in some ways, but it never extinguished her fire for being who she truly was. Volunteering with the Cherokee community during her residency was one of the most healing aspects of her journey. They understood what it was like to be distanced. This helped Natalie to embrace herself for who she truly was, gifts and all. It was so sad Mr. Bowden didn't have someone earlier in his life to give him that kind of courage or support. Now here he was, a middle-aged man, alone and trying to find out who he was. At least he has the sense to seek professional help, Natalie commended.

His session went well, she felt, with questions asked, revelations made, and new ways of thinking introduced. This was going to take time to reconstruct a personality. She scratched notes to remind herself of options she may want to pursue with his therapy.

Natalie continued to feel uneasy throughout the session, as flashbacks of nightmares randomly stole her concentration. The images of Jared made her stomach lurch. Just like it felt in the dream, she remembered. Mr. Bowden's thoughtfulness, coffee just the way she liked it, didn't help, either. The rest of the day's patients went much better, thankfully. She would work harder at releasing her energy before seeing a patient first thing–if she slept, that is.

The last patient for the day had cancelled, so Natalie took advantage and went for a run before it got dark. Early sunset was the thing she hated most about the winter months, but at least it had been unusually warm for February. She felt safe in the general vicinity of the Town Square where she lived because there was always activity and many people about. When she went for a run along the wooded path, she got nervous lately. The beautiful trails in North Carolina always brought her peace, but not today. Besides the nightmares, she had been feeling as though someone was watching. Learning to trust her instincts, instead of ignoring them like she had as a child, took conscious effort. Like her patient, Mr. Bowden, she had to learn to create new thought patterns and behaviors that validated who she was as opposed to who someone else told her to be.

Mindfully connecting to the energies of the trees, sky, and Earth, Natalie began at a slow jog to warm up. Feeling the energy moving through her body, releasing stress and freeing her mind, she picked up the pace and settled into a comfortable run, feeling more like herself. Just off the path ahead, a flock of birds were frightened out of their resting place for the evening. They scattered as she approached. Instantly, Natalie's intuition told her something wasn't right. A streak of panic shot through the center of her body as movement appeared in the direction from where the birds had come. Something large was in the woods, but thick brush and darkening shadows from the end of the day made it impossible to see clearly. Hoping to scare off a bear, Natalie stopped running and shouted, "Who's there!?" in the most forceful, intimidating voice she could muster. Bears were common in her neck of the woods and should hibernate in February. Her mind desperately needed it to be a bear and not a man hiding in the woods. Unfortunately, intuition told her otherwise.

Frozen with fear, Natalie let out a bloodcurdling scream as a bike rider rapidly ascended behind her on the path. Scaring the biker as much as herself, he ran into the brush where the movement had occurred. She could hear footsteps thumping on the ground and thrashing through the brush over the biker, who was trying to disentangle himself. The thought of pursuing the unknown fleeing entity flashed through Natalie's mind. She quickly realized how foolish that would be, having nothing to defend herself with and not even knowing for sure what the entity was. A bear could slash her to shreds and maul her… and so could a man. That last thought made her head spin as the realization of what almost happened struck her like a blow. Collapsing into a sitting position, Natalie choked back tears of anger, fear, and helplessness. The biker let go of his bike, sending it crashing to the ground as he ran to check on her.

"Hey! Are you okay!? You screamed and then collapsed! What's wrong?"

"Oh my God, I'm so sorry! I should ask YOU! I'm okay, just scared. There was something in the woods right where your bike ran into, and you scared it away!" Natalie hated how she sounded, like a scared little girl. She didn't like being, feeling, or appearing vulnerable.

"Yeah, I heard it! The bushes engrossed me to look. It sounded like someone running through the woods!"

He thought the same thing; that there was someone in the woods running away, Natalie thought to herself. Holy fucking shit! She panicked again.

"Do you think someone was hiding in there or going to attack you?" The biker's eyes were round as saucers as he realized what he had potentially prevented.

"I honestly do not know. I was hoping it was a bear, but it sounded more like a person. My intuition is screaming that you just saved me from God knows what! I am SO sorry I caused you to wreck! Are you okay?"

"Oh yeah, I'm fine. Just a few scratches from the branches and a flat tire. No big deal. How about we walk together since I can't ride and there's someone out there in the woods," he looked around as though wondering if someone was still out there watching them. "I'm Brian," he said, as he offered a hand to help her up.

"Natalie. And I owe you a new bike tire and a beer."

"No way! I got to save a damsel in distress! I'm a frigging knight in shining armor!" Brian had a wide smile and charming face as he joked to lighten the mood.

"This Damsel would prefer not to need a knight or saving, but I am beyond grateful that you came speeding in on your bike!" She was glad Brian had a sense of humor, too.

They joked and walked back to the Town Square, enjoying each other's company. Brian's girlfriend also had an apartment there, where he stored his bike for the great trails and paths nearby. Too bad he's got a girlfriend, Natalie pouted inwardly. They exchanged phone numbers in case he needed to be contacted for information to add to a police report. They hugged and promised to meet again for a beer under better circumstances. The hug elicited a quick thrill through her body and caused her to muse. Well, I've got his number, and he's got mine in case he finds himself single!

In the sanctity of her apartment, Natalie poured a hearty glass of her favorite red wine, grabbed Sage, and sank into the overstuffed chair. Clearly remembering what had happened before she contacted the police would be helpful. Sage purred, lavishing the attention, while Natalie let the taste of the wine linger in her mouth before enjoying its warmth. The warmth of the elixir slid down her throat, making her extra relaxed. Now she had to re-enact the scene, regardless of how frightening it would be. Closing her eyes, she concentrated on how her senses felt as opposed to what she saw.

Immediately, the uneasy sensation of being watched enveloped her. She had felt it before the birds flew off and alerted her to where someone was laying in wait. This person has watched me before, suddenly popped into her head. That was how she sometimes received messages and information and knew it to be accurate. Natalie would not make the mistake of doubting the information she was being given.

Okay, what else? she summoned to her Spirit Guides. She saw an image. Standing in her apartment and looking out the window. A sense of someone watching her ran through her veins. But who?

"It's the same person!" She shouted, opening her eyes in astonishment. "Oh my God, someone is stalking me! Who?!" she called out to the heavens, searching as though an Angel would appear and give her all the answers. Closing her eyes again and trying to connect to the Divine, Natalie did her best to calm her mind and her breathing to "hear and see." She just kept going back and forth between work and the night in the bar. Dammit, I can't get my concentration back and stay focused. I'm letting my own thoughts block information. I can't exactly tell the police, either, that my Spirit Guides showed me I'm being stalked! Knowing a report needed to be filed sooner than later, Natalie reached for her phone to call in and at least report the incident in the woods. Thank God Brian can back up that much of my story. Why is everything so confusing? Sometimes it feels like I'm walking between world's.

The police report was easy. Questions asked and answered. Brian's information was re-assurance they would make a police presence obvious in the vicinity. Natalie was still feeling helpless. Should this jack ass attack me, what good is a police report going to do? She argued with herself. They're going to look at my dead body and say "oh, hey look… someone was stalking her!" Rage in her bones coursing hot through her veins made Natalie seethe at how women were made out to be prey, besides the audacity men had at thinking women were theirs to do with as they pleased. Natalie caught herself in her thoughts. Daddy issues, little girl, she chided herself, vividly remembering how her domineering father dictated to her mother. Natalie could feel her father's need for complete control and her mother's submission. It fanned the flames of her existing anger. Yet, she knew on another level he was watching over her.

Using her skills as a trained Clinical Psychologist, Natalie did her best to emotionally detach from the situation. I've got a few things happening here, and I need to make sure my own emotional triggers aren't clouding my perceptions. First, the nightmares. They began after I worked with Ben and acknowledged my own gifts. Do they have anything to do with the fact I suppressed my abilities and now they're pouring out of my psyche with a vengeance as nightmares? Let's look at their theme; a domineering, abusive man keeping me captive. Is this a projection of my parents? My father wasn't physically abusive, but his authority held us all captive to a degree. Did my mother's weakness trigger my own feelings of anger, resentment, cowardice, and lack of control? Have I not dealt with these underlying concerns enough and now they are they are manifesting as nightmares? But what about the last one where I feel like I know the people I'm dreaming of? Who is the compassionate father-like figure and the jealous woman? Definitely not representative of my parents, but SO familiar! I've got three possibilities for the nightmares: stifled abilities, childhood trauma, or both. I can do something about those possibilities as a trained psychologist and can confront the nightmares. A small sense of calmness filled her mind and body as she failed to remember the physical trauma that lingered from her last two dreams.

The calmness quickly gave way to panic. What the hell do I do? She mused, not being willing to lie down and give in. Managing this issue was impossible. Attempting to calm a potentially irrational mind, Natalie perused the facts. She hadn't actually seen anyone watching her when she was looking out the window the day before. In the woods, she saw a figure and heard running footsteps, but didn't unquestionably see anyone then, either. I've got two incidents that have made me believe I have a stalker where I saw no one. Realizing how paranoid and ridiculous it all sounded, Natalie felt ashamed, like she had as a little girl, for crying over monsters in her dreams. It is just an overactive imagination; she heard her father chide in her head. "Okay, daddy," Natalie firmly responded to the imaginary conversation she had begun with her deceased father. "You didn't have gifts like I do and if you did, you didn't understand them just like I didn't all those years ago. That doesn't mean you're right and I don't give you permission to demean me or discount my abilities." Adult Natalie stood up for Little Natalie like she wished she could have done twenty-five years ago. Years of role playing, writing letters that would never be sent and healing the wounded child within herself, validated what she knew to be accurate, according to her intuition. Bolstering her own confidence, Natalie thought back over countless instances where she had relied on her gift of "knowing" and it had paid off. Every time. It was when she had doubted herself, she got into trouble. In her core, she could feel someone was watching and unsettling in her own mind. She had a stalker but couldn't prove it. Being aware is half the battle, right? She reasoned. So, what about the other half of this battle where you're in danger? Her alter ego interjected. Back to my original question, what the hell do I do?

Options flooded her mind. Moving in with a friend was one. She could get a gun or a taser, get a big dog, hire a bodyguard, she snorted as she laughed at that thought, put a camera up outside the front door, or have regular check-ins with someone. They were all sound ideas. Well almost all, but nothing solved the problem or the danger. The stalker had to be caught. As of right now I can't prove I have a stalker, so I have to protect myself in the meantime. A gun was out of the question. Growing up, she had shot rifles and pistols with her brother and his friends, but she never took care of her own gun or officially learned how to use one. Training courses were offered, but that required more time than she had. A taser or bear spray felt more reasonable. Ok next, a big dog. She loved animals but wasn't sure it was the best time to take on the responsibility of a dog. That's why she had an independent, self-sufficient cat! Sage even had a water fountain, a self-cleaning litter box and a self-feeder, which was undoubtedly why the kitty was "curvy"! Natalie grinned and wrinkled her nose adoringly at the thought of her voluptuous feline.

Oh my God, wait! Lisa's german shepherd, Natalie was Lisa's stand-in second mother for the gorgeous but protective pooch. As an artist, Lisa had aptly named her regal white german shepherd Monet. Any time Lisa needed a dog sitter, Monet would stay with Natalie. Being a very laid-back kitty, Sage was no fun for Monet to chase. The two usually just curled up together. Monet could accompany Natalie to work, as other therapists brought dogs in as therapy animals. That meant telling Lisa, though. Natalie's stomach lurched at the thought of Lisa's reaction.

Natalie would prefer to do daily check-ins with Lisa. She knew the conversation must be had, regardless of borrowing her dog. Besides, it was safer if friends knew she needed tabs to be kept on her. The thought of telling and worrying the gang brought about a whole new round of anxiety. Voicing what was happening also made it real. Natalie sat wide-eyed and transfixed, feeling as though she were about to jump off a bridge or something. Once a plan hatched, it would set events into motion and there was no telling how or what would unfold. Sticking her head in the sand wasn't an option, though. Closing her eyes and taking a deep breath, Natalie forced her thoughts to ponder what else she needed to do. One guy from their gang of friends could install a front door camera. The thought of leaving her apartment to stay with one of them instead was like gasoline on the rage that had died down to an ember. No fucking way was someone going to drive her out of her home. That's where I draw the line, she stubbornly declared.

Natalie's thoughts stopped short of Lisa. **THAT'S** what's unsettling me! Head spinning, short of breath, nausea enveloped Natalie as she remembered Lisa's new love interest, Jared.

Chapter 5

"Are you alone?" Natalie texted Lisa, hoping to catch her best friend without company.

"Is that a proposition, lol?" Lisa jokingly responded.

"I wish it were that fun. I need to talk."

Immediately, Natalie's phone rang. "What's wrong?" Lisa demanded with an equally concerned tone.

"I really didn't want to worry anyone, but I need help." Natalie's voice cracked as she struggled to get the complete sentence out.

"I'm on my way!"

"Ok," Natalie choked out. "Can you bring Monet and stay the night?"

"We'll stay as long as you need. Be right there.

Nat… I love you."

"I love you too. See you soon."

Natalie hung up and heaved with uncontrollable sobs. She hated to admit it, but fear combined with anger blanketed her emotions, leaving a feeling of helplessness that she couldn't stand. Asking for help was something alien to her. Accepting support from Lisa was different; she was more of a sister, but it left Natalie feeling vulnerable. She didn't know why that bothered her so much, it just did.

Swollen eyes and a red, runny nose greeted Lisa and Monet at the apartment door. Monet, sensing that her surrogate mommy was distressed, jumped up onto Natalie with her large front paws and licked at her tear-stained face. Relief immediately flooded Natalie's body as they collapsed together onto the floor, amidst much needed laughter and exchanged affection.

Sensing her friend did not need a lecture, Lisa reached out and hugged her tightly. Knowing she was not alone in her plight, Natalie let the anxiety drain from her limbs as Lisa supported her, stroking her hair and telling Natalie, "It's okay. I've got you. And I brought pizza."

They both broke into subdued laughter, knowing that no crisis was to be solved on an empty stomach.

"I hope I didn't interrupt anything," a worried

expression accompanied Natalie's beginning to an apology.

"Just an evening painting. I was hoping for an excuse not to eat an entire pizza alone. My thighs would give me away come summer!" They always made each other smile, no matter the circumstances. "I see you started drinking without me! I'm going to grab a glass, then we can sit down and talk while we eat. Is this about the nightmares?"

"Well, they certainly don't help the situation, but no, this is about something a bit more tangible. Kind-of. I mean, yes, I'm having nightmares and I'm trying to figure out their root cause, but in the mean-time something more serious has developed." The look on Lisa's face prompted Natalie to move along with divulging details, or her friend was going to join her in a panic attack. "Yesterday morning I had the feeling someone was watching me as I stood in the window. I heard 'You're mine' in my head. I jumped away from the window but saw no one. It was one of my episodes where something happens, and I just know." As her confidant growing up, Lisa was familiar with Natalie's abilities and understood how accurate her sense of knowing was. "This evening my last client cancelled, so I went for a run, thinking that there was enough daylight for it to be safe." Lisa's brows shot straight up, and her eyes hardened as thoughts raced ahead of what may have happened. "I saw a large figure hiding behind some brush off of the path. I screamed just as a biker came around the corner and caused him to accidentally run into the bushes. The figure ran off, but we both thought it was a person." An expression of horror and disbelief consumed Lisa's beautiful face.

"Do you think it was someone waiting for you in hiding?!"

"I meditated back to the incident and concentrated on what I felt before I saw the figure. I could feel someone watching me again and then a flock of birds suddenly flew off from where the person was hiding. That's how I saw where they were. Also, in my meditation, I was told that it's the same person."

Lisa's hands flew to her mouth as she gasped and then pounded the table with balled up fists. "Son of a bitch!" she screamed. Lisa was too angry that someone was threatening her "sister" to be scared. "Do you have any idea who it could be?"

"I honestly haven't got a clue." Natalie's mind darted to Jared and how her body reacted to him, but that made no sense. Until she had a firm grasp on why she was reacting so strangely to Jared, saying anything to Lisa didn't feel right.

"We've got to call the police!"

"I already filed a report about what happened in the woods. And I've got the name and number of the biker to back me up, but I've got no proof that I'm being stalked. You know how this works; I can't tell the police I'm a psychic medium and expect them to take me seriously."

Lisa rolled her eyes and combed her fingers through her hair. "Oh yeah. Why do I always forget about that?" she joked about herself.

"Because you've known me long enough to know I'm right about things and having no proof! Maybe someday intuition will be proof enough, but Western North Carolina will be the last place on Earth that happens! Right now, I need help to figure out what to do."

Lisa took it upon herself to send a group text out to their gang of childhood friends, apprising them of the situation. One by one, they showed up at Natalie's apartment, bringing food, beer, and a security camera for the front door. Monet was in heaven with all the attention and table scraps, while Sage retreated to the bedroom. Plans, some plausible, many outrageous yet funny, were tossed around. Natalie definitely was not alone, and her heart was as swollen with love and gratitude as her eyes were. She cried again because of the show of support taking place in her apartment and did her best to hide how overwhelmed she felt. Of course, she wanted them to know how grateful she was, but dammit, why did she have to cry? A lick on the face from Monet switched the soppy emotions to laughter.

Before everyone left, the camera was installed and hooked up to Natalie's cell phone for alerts. They also enabled her phone to share her location with them all, should she go missing. Natalie called her office receptionist and arranged for all appointments for the rest of the week to be rescheduled. She didn't feel as though she could do her clients justice by treating them in her current emotional state. Hopefully, a few days off would give her time to pull herself together. Lisa tidied the kitchen as Natalie readied herself for bed.

The king-sized bed, a gift from Natalie's last boyfriend, was almost too small for two grown women and a white German Shepherd. Monet always slept in the bed with Natalie when she was dog sitting, but Lisa was never there! They giggled, just as they had done having sleepovers as little girls. Natalie's anti-anxiety medicine kicked in and she plummeted into a deep slumber.

Monet's whining to go outside awoke Natalie mid-morning. Gently closing the bedroom door, she let Lisa sleep. Some things never change, she smiled to herself. Lisa had always slept hard and well into the late morning hours.

Donning a jacket over her pajamas and slipping

on her Nike's, Natalie headed downstairs with Monet for a quick spin around the small park in the middle of the Town Square. People who lived in the community did the same thing with their dogs. It wasn't unusual to see dog owners out in a variety of clothing. Monet quickly took care of business, besides greeting a few doggie friends and their owners. Enjoying herself, Natalie contemplated how having her own canine companion might be fun. For now, she was enjoying Monet and getting lost in chatting with people as they strolled around the park. She sure was the perfect protector, she thought.

Simultaneously, hackles rose up on Monet's back, just as the hair on the back of Natalie's neck stood up. Monet began scanning the perimeter, going into full protection mode as a low growl made it known she would attack if provoked. Natalie couldn't help but look around, scanning for a visible stalker. Since this was not part of her routine, she realized someone must have been waiting for her to appear. She couldn't decide if she was more angry or more afraid. Rather than giving the stalker a show, they headed back to Natalie's apartment on a roundabout route. She supposed he knew which apartment was hers, but why not try to throw him off, anyway.

Taking a different route, Natalie and Monet narrowed in on someone quickly ducking around a corner.

They ran to catch up just as an elevator closed its doors. Going up, Natalie took note, since they were already on the ground floor. Finding a nearby set of stairs, they ran as fast as they could to the next floor. The elevator doors stood open with the elevator empty. There was no one in sight. "Grr, they must have run away, Monet."

Fervently, she looked around for anyone who appeared suspicious. Nothing. Am I just being paranoid? No, Monet sensed it too, and my intuition was screaming at me as I was being watched. God, I want to stand here and scream too! I will not be a victim to anyone's game!

Mad, scared, and frustrated, Natalie led Monet back to her apartment. She hadn't been smart enough to take her phone. Checking it, there were several alerts about movement outside her door. Well, the camera works, she ruefully assessed. As far as the tracking on my phone, guess it won't work if I don't take it, smacking her forehead. "If someone had kidnapped me in my pajamas, my phone would still be sitting on my counter!" She angrily stated out loud, as Monet cocked her head to listen. As if understanding, Monet let out a soft bark to remind Natalie no one was going be kidnapped on her watch!

"What are you two talking about?" A sleepy Lisa appeared in the bedroom doorway, stroking a purring Sage.

"Let me get some coffee going and I'll tell you all about our morning adventure."

"An adventure already? But you're still in your pajamas!"

Monet barked again a little louder, as if to emphasize it was too early for that kind of adventure, but she was game.

"Are you fucking kidding me?" Lisa angrily exclaimed as Natalie conveyed what had happened in the Town Square. "Nat, we have got to call the police!"

"And tell them someone was in a hurry to get around a corner before I got there? Or that they left the elevator empty? Oh wait, Monet raised her hackles. That will have the police here in a jiffy!" Natalie wasn't angry with Lisa, but frustrated there was no solid proof to back up the fact she was in danger. This person was sly and mysterious, with a dark sense of humor.

Arms crossed and fuming, Lisa huffed and stared across the room. Narrowing her eyes, she got up and walked out onto the balcony, letting Monet come out with her. Natalie grabbed their coffees and joined her.

"Do you think he's watching?"

"I'm not feeling anything at the moment. Maybe it would be a good time for a run!" Natalie halfway joked.

Lisa punched her in the arm, sloshing their coffee. "You are NOT running anywhere unless it's in a heavily populated gym, young lady!"

"Crap, I'm going to lose what's left of my mind if I can't be outside! That's why I want to borrow Monet!"

"I was thinking she would help protect you at work and in your apartment! Not something stupid like running in the woods!"

"It's a designated, well-used path designed for the neighborhood community. You make it sound like I'd be off by myself in the middle of nowhere."

"Yes, a path he's already found AND stalked you on! Are we really having this conversation?"

"No." Natalie sighed. "I'm just wishful thinking. I'm pissed. And scared. And I want my life back! Obviously, this person knows where I live and that's creepy."

"Well, you didn't have a nightmare last night, did you? That's a start."

"Huh, you're right! For a moment I forgot about those! I guess having you and Monet as bed buddies solves that problem! Who needs boyfriends or future husbands?!"

"Speaking of which… not that he's a boyfriend or a future husband, but Jared and I were going to catch a movie here in the Town Square tonight. Interested?"

Natalie sputtered in her coffee. "Oops, went down the wrong way!" she lied, trying to conceal the reaction. It was a good thing Lisa chose not to tune in to her own intuition or Natalie could never hide the strange feelings toward Jared. "Absolutely not. You two enjoy your evening."

"I'll cancel, then. No way I'm leaving you."

"We haven't talked about any of this long term. I'm praying that this is over sooner than later, but I do NOT want a babysitter! Thank you from the bottom of my heart for being here for me, but this is my problem and I've got to handle it."

"So, if the situation were reversed, would you leave me?"

Natalie frowned and gave Lisa a pout.

"I didn't think so. There's safety in numbers, so two of us… three actually, counting Monet, are safer together."

"Let's look at the reality of this. I've got to go back to work next week. I'm gone all day and I'll be around people. My apartment is in a huge development, constantly full of activity. I can scream and someone will come running. It's also patrolled by security. Besides, if you let me borrow Monet, she will be with me at all times, except for something like going to the grocery store. It's not like your situation where you live in a house where no one sees you coming and going. I'm literally surrounded! We've got a plan in place and maybe this stalker guy will get bored and move on. Please, go home, paint, and run your gallery. Monet and I will be just fine! I'm going to get bear spray in every size so I can have some with me no matter where I am!" Natalie hoped she sounded more assured than she really felt. She didn't want to be alone, but she didn't want to be hindered by someone else constantly around, either.

Lisa squinted her eyes as she weighed Natalie's argument. Arms crossed, drumming the fingers on her right hand, she stuck her chin up and countered. "I'll compromise. Today is Wednesday and you have the rest of the week off. I'll stay here with you and Monet through the weekend. Monday, we both go back to work. I go home, leaving Monet with you. We'll see how it goes during the week and take it from there. Deal? Oh, and I'll go to a movie tonight with Jared. It will be nice to just walk down to the Square instead of having to drive!"

Knowing that there was little to no room to argue, Natalie stuck her hand out to shake on their deal. Smiling, they hugged instead.

"I've got two things I need to do today. One is walking down to REI and deplete them of their bear spray supply and the other is to go see Ben. I was going to consult with him on Saturday, but I'm hoping he can help me see what the hell is happening, so I want to go today. I'll take Monet."

"Ok. I'll see you safely on your errand to REI and then watch y'all leave for the Reservation. I'll go take care of some things at the gallery while you're gone. I've got your spare key to your apartment, so I can bring a few more things over as well."

With a temporary plan in place, they set about their day. Armed to the teeth with bear spray, Natalie and Monet began the long drive to the Cherokee Reservation. She had texted Ben ahead of time to double check he was available to see her.

Driving into the Reservation, Natalie relaxed and felt as though she had come home. Once she got past the tourist attraction section of town, the chaos faded, and she could feel the trees and the Earth welcoming her back. A bald eagle screeched overhead, angry that an Osprey wouldn't share its catch. Deer off the side of the road turned their ears towards them, assessing the big white animal in the car. Monet met their stares with equally tuned ears and interest. Winding her way to Ben's house, Natalie knew she was safe there. The Reservation was her sanctuary where she had learned so much, including who she truly is. The knowledge and wisdom Ben had brought was beyond astounding and something that was never taught growing up religiously. If only more people knew the ancient wisdom available, they would be more in tune with their own soul nature. Parking the car in front of Ben's house, she and Monet jumped out to stretch as relief settled into her body.

"Ah, my fledgling has returned to the nest," she heard Ben call from the front porch. A warm, embracing hug melted all worries away as they all entered the house. Natalie was smiling on the inside and outside to be in the comfort of this familiar old soul.

"Thank you for seeing me today," Natalie implored as she kept a hand wrapped around Ben's arm. He patted her arm as they walked into his house. "You always make me feel so safe and comfortable." Ben just nodded.

"There is nothing more important to me than to be of help, my dear," the tanned, older yet handsome man replied as he turned and peered into Natalie's soul. "I see your torment, feel your angst and share your concern. It is good that you have a protector," he smiled, looking down at Monet. "She will not leave you." Ben tossed a tanned piece of meat to Monet as they sat down at the kitchen table to talk. His place was not luxurious by any means and had a stench from the earth. Definitely not the best housekeeper. However, the artifacts were intriguing from his heritage, especially the amulet around his neck.

There was no need for Natalie to convey what had happened, but she did anyway, for the sake of getting it off her chest. It was oddly therapeutic to confide in someone that made her feel safe. It was as though she handed her emotions to a trusted ally who would know what to do with them. Ben was the father she had needed growing up. He listened closely, nodding his head, and knew things in the same way that Natalie did.

"Let us walk with this."

Grateful for the opportunity to be outside, they walked through the woods to a small creek that ran alongside Ben's property, she noticed a white feather on the trail. Natalie stopped, closed her eyes and breathed in the smell of the sweet birch, poplar and maples trees, all gifts from the Earth. Listening to the gentle song of the water as it trickled across polished stones, her mind began to relax. I know someone is watching over me every time those feathers show up. It's quite interesting when they do try to give me a sign or message. I must pay more attention, she thought.

As Ben had taught her, Natalie invited Nature to be one with her, sharing its strength, lessons, and wisdom. She finally broke the silence, "I know there are messages from the trees, the animals and the water, but I need deeper guidance than what they offer. What do you know, Ben?"

He motioned to a bench which was crafted from an old oak tree. "Come sit." Monet investigated all the new smells, while keeping a watchful eye on Natalie.

"You have done battle with this enemy many times. He is a wolf in sheep's clothing that walks with you through time. Your strength has not been great enough to defeat him until now. The work you have done in this lifetime will enable you to end this now, but it will be dangerous. Great Spirits also walk with you, offering their guidance and protection. Call upon them in time of need." Monet laid down at her feet. "Another Evil seeks you out. The man with two faces lives in the shadows. Your souls have not crossed paths before in time. His energy is in need and yours offers a light that he cannot find within himself."

"I have TWO stalkers?!" Natalie was incredulous. "I've only felt one in my meditation!"

"Perhaps the second has not yet revealed himself, but he is there. Be wary and listen to your intuition. Your

Soul will tell you who he is. It is your path to do battle with him. It is up to you to use your skills to win this time."

"Wow, I've got to get busy honing in those gifts, then! I hope bear spray and a door camera will help!" she tried to lighten the mood.

"I have something for you." Ben pulled out an amulet hanging from a sterling silver chain. "It is for protection. Wear it and know I walk with you."

Tears welled up in Natalie's brilliant blue eyes, made even more electric from crying–again. It was similar to the one Ben wore, but smaller. Natalie was feeling quite honored and overwhelmed with this gift. She knew it was truly a gift. "Dammit, what is with all of this crying!" She complained as he fastened the necklace for her.

"It is your soul acknowledging the gifts which bring you love. No tear is ever unnecessary or wasted."

"Well, now I feel kind-of shitty for getting mad at them," she joked.

"Your sensitivity is one of your greatest strengths, and greatest weakness. Be aware of necessary boundaries to protect yourself. Not all are as they appear. Perhaps a run would do your mind, body and soul good."

"How can you read me so incredibly well?" She asked, astonished at Ben's perception.

"We, too, have spent many lifetimes together. I know you well. We reincarnate to remember and to finish out what was incomplete." Smiling, Ben began walking back to his house. "You are safe here. Be one with nature. She welcomes your energy."

Not so oddly, Natalie had worn exercise clothes, hoping to spend time outside. With a grin on her face, she and Monet set off for a jog, embraced in the Reservation's refuge.

The drive home was just long enough for her to digest that there were two stalkers. Determination replaced anxiety as she weighed Ben's revelations in her mind. I know I've been slowly working on acknowledging and developing my gifts. Like Ben has said, skills are like muscles; they have to be used in order to be strengthened. I wonder what the circumstances have been in past lives that kept me from being strong enough to fight back? Lost in a reverie, she ignored the notifications on her phone about the front door camera.

Chapter 6

On pins and needles, Natalie had a foreboding sensation in her gut. Was it because she was home, where the stalker knew she lived, or because something was going to happen? Too bad "gifts" don't work the way people assume they do. You can't just see what's going to happen. If that were the case, I'd have seen the numbers to the winning lottery ticket and be on vacation somewhere exotic with a bodyguard–or ten, she mused, parking the car. The thought of leaving was tempting, but where would she go? She had to come home sometime, so she and her canine bodyguard made their way through the desolate parking garage.

Grateful for Monet's watchful eyes and the large can of bear spray in her hand, she unlocked the door to the apartment. Lisa called out a greeting as Monet positioned herself in front of Natalie and began ferociously barking at

Jared. Teeth bared and hackles raised, she was a force to be reckoned with. Natalie did not expect Jared and Lisa's date would begin at her apartment, so did not foresee coming face to face again with him in her own living room.

Ben's amulet around her neck suddenly felt hot as it glowed. What is my soul trying to communicate about Jared? Now Monet apparently senses something, too, and the amulet has come to life! The faint scent of his cologne intoxicated Natalie's senses, eliciting an irresistible thrill of sensual hunger, catching her off guard, yet familiar, deep within her soul.

Natalie's thoughts flashed back to her strange, visceral reaction when she saw Jared in the bar and again whenever she thought about him. Confused and not sure what to do, Natalie stood still as Lisa scolded her beautiful dog.

Monet wavered between wanting to obey her owner and protect her friend. Placing her purse on the floor, Natalie sat down beside her defender, stroking her fur, talking soothingly to her, and thanking Monet for keeping her safe while desperately trying to distract her mind and body's awareness of Jared's presence. Monet reluctantly ceased the aggressive behavior, but never let her eyes waver from Jared, indicating he was not coming near Natalie without being bit.

"What the hell is happening with her?!" Lisa was both angry and embarrassed.

"Maybe she's taking her job too seriously," Natalie tried a tentative smile, trying to diffuse the charged energy in the room.

Turning to Jared, Lisa offered an apology, lost as to what her crazy dog was thinking.

"Well, she's used to seeing me at your house, not here where she's got a job to protect someone, I guess." Jared shifted his gaze from Lisa to Monet and then bored a hole through Natalie as his gaze turned into a smoldering conveyance of passion.

Oblivious, Lisa's attention was still on her dog, whom she continued to berate.

New sensations erupted within Natalie as she met Jared's emotion with uncontrollable fire in her wild eyes. Her body responded, sending a surge of desire up through her core, pushing Natalie's senses out of control and overriding any warnings intuition had given her.

Jared could detect Natalie's response and was in danger of losing his self-control. He fervently wanted Lisa and Monet to leave so he could take Natalie to where they had gone together in his fantasies. His dreams about Natalie were erotic; she drove him with lust to the point of madness. The hold she had on him since their introduction in the bar was unsettling as he perseverated over her, desperately needing to consume this sensual creature. Jared had sensed Natalie's attraction to him, but also sensed her loyalty to Lisa. He didn't care; she wants me as much as I want her; I can feel it and nothing is going to stop us, he solemnly swore.

Jared attempted to remain in Natalie's company by suggesting they all go grab dinner in the Town Square together. "It will give Monet time to relax while we have a little fun and then we can go to the movie."

"That's a great idea," Lisa jumped at the suggestion. "Nat, even if you just want to grab a bite and skip the movie, that's an option too!" she politely amended, suddenly remembering how Jared had made advances towards Natalie when they met in the bar.

"Thanks guys, but I am going to spend a peaceful evening here relaxing right along with Monet. I haven't been sleeping well and could use some rest." She excused herself, knowing Lisa would detect the intense vibes being exchanged around her. I will not let a guy destroy our friendship, regardless of how insane he makes me feel. She committed to herself. Jared's disappointment was palpable as Natalie stood up. "Goodnight!" she cheerily called, hastily making her way to the bedroom. "I won't wait up for you!"

Closing the bedroom door behind her, Natalie nearly collapsed as the weight of the intense emotions she just experienced overwhelmed her. She could still feel Jared's emotional pull from behind the closed door.

"Goodnight!" she heard Lisa reply as the apartment door closed behind them.

Natalie sank to the floor, breathing erratically, eyes wild yet again, and began rocking back and forth while wrapping her arms around her knees. Oh my God, oh my God, oh my God!!! What do I do? What the fuck do I do?!?! Monet rested her head on Natalie's shoulder. Turning around and wrapping her arms around the pup's neck, she hugged tightly as if it were her sole source of support. Realizing that without Lisa, that actually was the case, Natalie became alarmed. "Monet, Lisa is all I've got! It's obvious her boyfriend and I have intense chemistry, but I would never act on that! It would cost me the most important friendship I have! I'm going to avoid him. I'll have to make excuses to Lisa and hopefully she'll tire of him soon."

Feeling as though her head and heart may explode with the irresistible draw to Jared, Natalie made her way back out to her favorite overstuffed chair. Mindlessly rubbing Ben's amulet between her thumb and forefinger, she summoned help from her Angels and Spirit Guides.

Eyes closed, Natalie breathed deeply down into her abdomen, allowing her heart to slow its frantic pace and her mind to clear from the shock and fright. "I call my Spirit back to connect with me mind, body, heart and soul," she murmured, as her soul settled deeply into her body, feeling as though a weighted blanket had been placed over her. Ben had taught her that as humans, we easily lose touch with our Divine essence, especially when we become emotional, and to call her Spirit back frequently. I am a Divine Soul having a human experience, she reminded herself. God and I made this plan together and together we will get through it. Show me what I need to know, Natalie requested with eyes closed, while using the vision of her third eye, or the mind's eye.

Instantly, flashes from nightmares appeared; a gentle man, a jealous woman and a torturer, ending with an image of Jared. The emotion within his crazed eyes revealed rage, possessiveness, jealousy, insanity, and an overwhelming desire to consume Natalie. I could feel madness emanating from Jared's energy. Her logical mind was overruling the meditation as thoughts and questions began firing in her brain. What has Jared got to do with my nightmares? And what are these disturbing feelings associated with him? Desperately attempting to regain the connection, Natalie breathed deeply and tried to keep her mind's eye open. Jared consumed her visions. It was no use for her to see anything else. My intense, irresistible attraction to him is clouding everything. I'm going to have to process this first before I can move on to the next stalker. She relented.

Allowing herself to return to the present moment, Natalie pulled a notebook and pen from the side table to jot down thoughts. A tremor from having been so deeply unnerved made her hand shaky. Wine first was a physical need more than a thought. I hope a glass of wine every night doesn't mean a dependency; she fretted but shoved the thought away as soon as it developed. I've got some serious shit to digest; give me a break, she argued with herself.

Settling back into the chair, Sage helpfully jumped into Natalie's lap. "Oh, well, hello! I guess I've neglected you a bit." After stroking Sage's soft fur and a few sips of wine having made its way through her extremities, Natalie was ready to put her thoughts in order. Setting the wine on the side table, she balanced the notepad on the arm of the chair so as not to disturb the gentle purrs of her current form of stress relief. With Monet sacked out at her feet, she began the task. Headlining the page with the title Nightmares/Jared, she used bullet points to mark each thought or question.

Ben's words; A wolf in sheep's clothing. He walks

through time with me. We have done battle many times. I'm strong enough to end it now. Will be dangerous.

Ben's additional warning; Another Evil seeks you out. The man with two faces lives in the shadows.

In my meditation; I saw flashes of recent nightmares and then Jared's face. I could feel his overwhelming emotions.

I had weird feelings when I met Jared and when I think about him. What is my intuition telling me??

Am I sensing Jared's attraction and mistaking it for being watched by someone?

Who is the man with two faces? Is he the one I've been feeling watching and who was in the woods?

Am I feeling both of them?

My meditation was the only time I've felt negative emotion surrounding Jared. In person, I feel a magnetic attraction.

How do I tell Lisa?? DO I tell Lisa?? Can I be honest and talk it out or would it end the friendship?

Realizing neither she nor Monet had eaten dinner, Natalie put aside the notebook and gently transferred Sage from her lap to the chair. Leftovers from when the gang had brought food made for an unhealthy dinner, but Natalie didn't have the energy to go to the grocery store.

She had no appetite anyway and was more concerned about feeding Monet. They went down to the park in the middle of the Town Square after Monet had eaten. Looking around, Natalie wondered which restaurant Lisa and Jared had gone to and if they could see her. The uneasy feeling of eyes watching crept up her neck, sending goose bumps down her arms. She pulled Monet away and wandered further down to a different grassy area that was a bit more private. Even though it was a Wednesday evening, the Square was still full of restaurant and movie goers and shoppers. Too busy for someone to try something, Natalie reasoned. Besides, Jared is with Lisa, so something's not right about my meditation. He's not a stalker. The sound of a low, guttural growl tore Natalie's attention from her thoughts.

Monet bolted from her side and sprinted towards an open area between the YMCA and some shops, dragging the leash behind her. Instinctively, Natalie sprinted after her, still in her running shoes from earlier in the day. Not caring for her own safety, Natalie screamed for Monet, terror filling her that something might happen to her beloved protector. Sounds of a car's screeching tires pointed Natalie toward a parking lot where she found Monet barking fervently after a dark sedan speeding away, past Mission Hospital where her office was. Breathless both from running and from the terror coursing through her body, Natalie fell to her knees when she reached Monet and sobbed uncontrollably, reaching out for Monet to come to her. Soft fur and a strong sense of loyalty filled her hands. Helplessness filled her senses as Natalie realized someone was constantly keeping her under surveillance. Not having the strength physically or emotionally to move, Natalie sat in the parking lot while she attempted to gain control over her panic. Finally, a security guard on patrol came by.

"Ma'am, are you in trouble?" The guard sounded as panicked as she felt. No one ever expects there to be trouble in an upscale neighborhood. The security guards are more for show than anything.

"My dog ran after someone that I think may have been following me," she feebly answered.

"They sped away in a dark-colored sedan. I didn't get any details about the car or see them. Worrying about my dog distracted me."

"Holy Mother of Jesus!" The guard fumbled with his radio as he went to call in the incident.

"Listen, I've been through more than I can handle today. Can I give you my contact information and file a report or whatever you need to do later? I just want to go home."

Appearing wary of dealing with an emotional

woman and questionable whether he could even properly fill out a report, the security guard gladly obliged to Natalie's request.

As if on autopilot, the two made their way back to the apartment. Natalie numbly unlocked the door and entered, noticing once again she had left her phone on the counter.

Quickly showering and taking an anxiety pill, Natalie considered the effectiveness of two instead. Praying one would work, she and Monet pulled themselves into bed, ready for the day to be over. Reaching out, stroking her fur and looking into the soulful eyes of the gentle soul that had twice saved her, Natalie thanked Monet for keeping her safe. "I love you, beautiful girl," whispered from her lips as she fell sound asleep. The next nightmare would offer deeper clues.

Chapter 7

"Maalik, I wish to go with you to sell your spices!" Bahara pleaded, imploring him with light hazel eyes that shone as though illuminated from behind.

"My dear niece, you know a woman's place is in the house! I would be killed for taking you and you would be beaten to death!"

Her husband's uncle, Maalik, was Bahara's required male escort today to the market, whose company she actually enjoyed. He preferred men, but was extremely discreet as to his sexual proclivities. For that reason, her husband, Abdul, allowed them to spend time together. Maalik did not treat her with disdain, as most men treated women, but as a friend. They walked slowly to have time to talk. He shared stories of his travels to Africa and various ports of call, selling his spices. It was rare for a man to treat a woman as a companion, and she felt as though she had known and adored him all her life. Perhaps he was the only friendly face she had known for the past six months since her arranged marriage and clung to his geniality.

"But Abdul is so cruel. He has his way with me in front of the other wives, making them watch. Then he holds me by my hair and beats me for not knowing what to do in the bed. I never saw my father treat my mother that way, but I know she hid things from me. I have heard stories of other women and their husbands, fathers, or other family members doing atrocious things and worse. I find myself one of them, abused with no life ahead of me or my unborn child!" A teardrop slowly slid down her tanned, youthful face, disappointed and frightened for her own life.

Repulsion emanated from Maalik's face. He made a sound as if he was going to vomit, regretting willful ignorance of his nephew's behavior. Stopping beneath a tree to steady himself, Maalik confessed, "I have heard rumors, but never saw evidence of this! Whenever I visit, all appears harmonious within his household!"

Sweat trickled down her back beneath her burqa as Bahara dared to look around while Maalik talked. She attempted to take mental notes of the layout of the qal'ah whenever they walked along the dusty roads. In Afghanistan, villages consisted of stone and mud-brick dwellings made from materials that would withstand the harsh temperatures of both winter and summer. The qal'ah, or fortress, consisted of walls surrounding the dwellings. It belonged to the family of the husband she had been forced to marry. Almost sixteen years old now, she was pregnant with her first child for roughly four months, as far as she could tell. As her husband's third wife, she had no priority within the household, not that women had rights in Afghanistan, anyway.

"Maalik, you are blessed not to follow the expected behaviors of adult men! This is how many of them are raised! Since you have never taken a wife nor wanted one, perhaps that has protected you from understanding," Bahara wisely counseled. "My marriage to Abdul was to form an alliance, however I am but a pawn with no hope of divorce. My absolute obedience is demanded by law, as I am voiceless with no chance of receiving any education other than what my mother secretly taught me and my sister. When I was a young girl, I witnessed a woman publicly beaten in our qal'ah for speaking to the grocer. From that young age, I have behaved as though I don't exist. All a man needs is the slightest excuse to beat or kill me! Maalik, what if my child is a girl?! I cannot allow a child to grow up here! I must escape!"

Maalik hung his head, placing one hand to his chest while sharply inhaling. "Oh, my dear niece, I am sorry! So very sorry and ashamed!" Keeping eyes closed and his head bowed, Maalik confessed, "There is no honor in my behavior. As a male, I have enjoyed life willfully disregarding the treatment of women in this country. I may not make the rules, but I enjoy the freedoms they offer me with no regard for the cost you pay." Eyes reflecting shame opened and pleaded with Bahara for redemption. "At a young age, I lost my mother and have no sisters for me to consider. My heart has remained aloof until your radiance stirred protective emotion I never knew existed. Were I to have had a child, I pray she would be like you. However, your words of truth strike terror in my heart! How can any man have a daughter and allow her to be treated with such cruelty?! How can he permit his own mother to be viewed as vermin?! I understand I do not hold the same views as a normal man in Afghanistan, however, I am far from normal!" A wink of an eye played at self-directed humor.

Wanting desperately to wrap her arms around Maalik, imagining she would feel comforted and protected in his paternal-like embrace, Bahara painfully kept all forbidden display of emotion to herself. "You would be the finest father, Maalik," she whispered as tears again streaked her face, alarmed that they, still, could draw attention to their conversation.

Concern emanated from Maalik's eyes as he desperately wished he could comfort the young girl he had grown so fond of. Confused by the affection and protectiveness he felt, Maalik resigned himself to help Bahara escape.

From the kitchen in the back of the house, the wives were dutifully preparing the evening meal. Bahara could hear Maalik and Abdul's voices. Since women were not permitted in the front of the house, Bahara strained to eavesdrop by the doorway.

"I wish to take another wife," she could hear Abdul say. "There is a girl I will have, but I must travel to make the arrangement with her father. I shall be gone two nights. Will you oversee the household in my absence?"

Bahara gasped in astonishment at the miracle that was presenting itself. This would be the ideal opportunity for her to escape! One of the other wives, Sabra, suspiciously watched the newest young bride who had stolen her coveted standing as the most youthful of the wives. Bahara wrapped her arms around her swollen belly, feigning to be ill from her pregnancy so she could continue to monitor the men's conversation. Unsympathetic, Sabra made a sound of impatience, appraised Bahara disdainfully with a flick of her eyes, and went about making the naan without Bahara's help.

"Of course, nephew," she could hear Maalik respond. "What is it you need with another new wife so soon? You must be exhausted keeping up with four!"

She could hear them laugh grotesquely and make vulgar remarks.

"I am unhappy with Bahara. She does not please me. Were she not pregnant already, I would dispose of her. I will wait to see the sex of the child and then I shall determine if I am disposing of one or two useless females."

Unable to breathe, Bahara fell to the floor in distress, her head making a sickening thud upon hitting the solid ground. It sounded as though a river was running through her ears as she lost vision and then consciousness.

Bahara's body reflexively jumped as she awoke in the shared bedroom alone, except for Maalik. He put his finger to his mouth, indicating she remain quiet upon regaining consciousness.

"I will get you out tomorrow night!" Maalik urgently whispered. "We shall meet when the moon is highest in the sky outside in the courtyard. Dress warmly, as a man." He patted her hand and kissed her on the forehead.

Bahara acknowledged his gestures of concern and

remained silent as he left.

She could hear him address Abdul as he went out into the front room. "Now that I know she is well, I can leave in peace, assured I will not be held to blame for the illness of your wife!"

"It would be no loss, Uncle!" Abdul cruelly retorted.

With thoughts colliding in her head, Bahara nearly passed out again. I must be strong and clever, she commanded herself. Carefully arising from the mattress on the floor, she snuck into Abdul's room to steal clothes for travelling. She placed them behind an urn in the courtyard so she could dress to travel when Maalik came for her. Grateful the other wives were still in the kitchen cleaning up after the evening meal, she offered to finish their task. Without acknowledging her, they left, casting scornful glances as they made their contempt obvious. Sabra intentionally bumped Bahara's shoulder hard as she passed by. Bahara smiled to herself. I will be the one free from this pit of despair while you foolishly try to please the devil!

She stored what food was left in rags, placing it behind supplies in the kitchen for her journey. It was hard to imagine what lie ahead for herself and her unborn child, but doing nothing meant imminent death.

It was seldom Abdul left, but when he did, the energy within the house was more relaxed. Tension was gone, and the wives spoke freely, smiling and occasionally laughing. Maalik checked in, making sure all was taken care of, but left the women to do as they please.

"You will travel out of the country by horse under the cloak of night," he whispered to Bahara while pretending to scold her for not doing the wash properly. "I have paid for your escape. Do not let anyone tell you otherwise. Take what you can with you. It will be a long, tumultuous journey. It is fortunate that we are in the southernmost region of Afghanistan. You will be taken through Pakistan to a port where one of my ships will transport you to Africa. I shall meet you there and ensure your establishment."

Bahara began to cry tears of gratitude. Sabra took notice, so Maalik pretended to scold her yet again, giving feigned reason for the tears.

"I shall be here tonight," he affirmed before walking away.

It was not unusual for Bahara to rise multiple times during the night with an infant in her belly pressing down upon her bladder. None of the wives or their children gave notice when she slipped off the communal mattress. Heart pounding, she silently made her way to the courtyard and donned Abdul's stolen clothing with trembling hands. Maalik came for her as promised. Before they could leave, a sound near the back entrance of the house startled them. Sabra stood in the shadows. Deliberately approaching, she spat on the ground, moonlight revealing a malicious sneer.

"You traitorous snakes are worthy of each other's company! May the wolves feast from your flesh!"

As if on cue, a wolf Bahara secretly fed scraps to, appeared in the courtyard searching for handouts. It stood defensively in front of Bahara, dense hair on the back of its neck raised, as it bared dangerously sharp incisors at Sabra, forcing her to back away.

"Perhaps it shall feast on *you!*" Bahara retorted as they nervously backed towards the courtyard and exited into the street. Turning its head, the wolf looked deeply into Bahara's eyes, holding her gaze as if conveying a message. Bahara silently thanked the animal as she and Amir turned and ran for the hidden entrance within the walls of the qal'ah and escaped, knowing there was nothing Sabra could do to stop them.

Two men awaited with horses at the base of the mountains to escort Bahara and three other women to a port in Pakistan. Donkeys carried bags full of supplies for the long, desolate quest. Bahara recognized one of the women as a girl from her own qal'ah who was slightly younger and had hope more girls would seek refuge.

Time could not be lost as the moon peaked, signaling daylight was mere hours away. Bahara threw her arms around Maalik, her heart heavy with both excitement and tremendous sorrow. He held her head close to him , kissing her on the forehead. He uttered a prayer to Allah to keep her safe. Then he assisted her upon the horse.

"I can never repay you, Maalik," she sobbed, reaching down to hold his hand one last time.

"You are my redemption for willfully disregarding the evil that has crept into the hearts of men. I will see you at the Port where we shall sail together to a new life." Tears swam in his gentle eyes as his voice trembled, and he patted her hand before stepping away. "Be safe, my child."

Bahara nodded, unable to speak further from the constriction in her throat as she wept, tears threatening to blind her.

The small caravan began their ascent into the mountains. Bahara looked around one last time at the land she wished to never see again. Her only sorrow was leaving behind Maalik and worry for her mother and sister, guilt creeping into her consciousness for leaving them behind. *I have no choice*, she reminded herself with a heavy heart. *Abdul means to kill me after our child is born. I must flee.* Overriding her emotion, Bahara steeled herself for the harrowing journey ahead.

A month and a half later, the weary caravan made their way towards the port where they had been instructed to rendezvous with Maalik. The men leading the mission were to receive the second half of their substantial payment for their transport services and their silence. Nervously, they all boarded the docked ship, awaiting their arrival. Maalik appeared from the ship's hold, his face pained as he reluctantly approached the travelers. Behind him, Abdul followed, dramatically pulling his sword from its scabbard, wearing a sinister scoff; as though fate was his to designate and triumph over. Nearly delirious from her journey, Bahara's mind frantically grasped to comprehend what was happening. *Is this a cruel mirage?* She pleaded to herself as she searched Maalik's face for hope.

"Look at ME you whore!" Abdul vehemently spat at Bahara.

Transfixing her gaze on the devil, she conveyed every emotion save for the one Abdul was sure he would find; fear. Her fate sealed, begging for mercy would benefit no one. She would not die a coward, but with courage. What she did not expect was the swift commotion aboard the ship's deck. A monkey scrambled from the cargo hold; an escaped pet belonging to a deckhand, smuggled from Africa. First jumping atop a crate and then leaping through the air, it landed on Abdul's head, gouging his left cheek as it catapulted itself from the ship to the dock. Finding freedom from captivity, commotion followed in its wake. Combat between Abdul and Maalik over the dropped sword ensued as Bahara and the two other women watched helplessly, alarmed that their own lives could soon end violently. Weak from malnourishment and elongated travel, their desperation peaked as Abdul gained control of the sword, aiming it for Maalik's throat.

Chapter 8

"NOOOOOOO!!!!!!!" Wailing and screaming, Natalie woke herself, remembering every detail of the nightmare. "NO, no, no, no!" she choked, knees pulled up to her chest, arms wrapped tight around them as she rocked back and forth in her bed sobbing. She could see Maalik's eyes; they seemed familiar. Natalie experienced the emotions of the nightmare as if she had been there. Her heart felt as though it was being ripped from her chest as Abdul sliced Maalik's throat. "Oh, God!" she cried, running for the bathroom. Heaving over the toilet, she violently vomited as agony consumed her body. Gasping for air while lying on the cool tile of the bathroom floor, Natalie saw into the soul of Abdul's eyes. A sadistic energy and need for domination emanated from them, taking Natalie back to a place in time she couldn't quite pinpoint. A fresh wave of nausea enveloped her body as she dry heaved to the point of passing out, the unforgiving tile meeting her head.

With no idea how long she had been lying unconscious on the cold floor, Natalie opened her eyes. Cautiously pulling herself to her feet, she filled the bathroom glass with cold water and sipped carefully, hoping it would stay down.

Sage jumped on the bathroom counter, startling Natalie and forcing her back to reality. The sight of the cat led her to the next question; *Where is Monet?* The unnerving nightmare had left her oblivious to the current circumstances. Monet should be right by me! Frantic, she started calling for her protective guardian. The bedroom door flung open, she scanned the living and dining area with no sign of Lisa or Monet. Perplexed, she noticed that Monet's food bowls were gone, as well as Lisa's belongings. *What the hell?* The notebook she had been writing in last night was no longer on the table by the chair, but was lying on the dining room table. Natalie's stomach fell to her feet as she remembered having made a list of Jared and the nightmares.

Her body trembled with dread, approaching the notebook as if it were a snake that would strike. Oh, please God, tell me Lisa didn't see what I wrote! How could I be so stupid to leave it laying out?! Already emotional and physically exhausted from her morning upheaval, Natalie wasn't sure she could handle another ordeal. Lisa's handwriting on a piece of paper lay across the top of the notebook, still turned to the page containing Natalie's writing from the night before.

"Wow, Nat, I never expected something like this from you," it read. "Working with crazy people has made you crazy, too. You don't even know Jared. How dare you accuse him of these insane things! You have weird emotions when you think of him?? What the hell are you doing thinking of MY boyfriend? Go get your own fucking boyfriend and leave mine AND ME the hell alone! Oh, and MY dog, too!"

Alarm seized her heart as Natalie thought about losing her best friend. Anger also flared at the thought of how ridiculous Lisa was behaving. She knows me better than anyone and fucking knows I am in danger and not chasing her boyfriend! How dare she react without talking things over first!

As she reached for her phone to call Lisa, a scratching at the door halted Natalie and made her check the front door camera instead. White fur covered the picture. Confused, she opened the door with caution, only to have Monet charge past her and into the apartment. "Oh my God, Monet, what are you doing here?!" Tears streamed down Natalie's face as she realized Monet must have escaped from Lisa and run across town to continue her job of protecting Natalie. Feeling guilty, but happy to have her beloved guardian angel back, she sat down on the floor and hugged the shepherd with great enthusiasm.

Ben's prophetic words echoed in her mind, "She will never leave you."

"I'm thinking Lisa is not going to take this very well."

Choosing to text and test the waters, Natalie sent Lisa a message, "Monet came back to my apartment. She is fine. Can we talk?" She waited with her heart in her throat for a response.

"You two traitors deserve each other," was Lisa's irrational response.

Anger flared again as Natalie reminded herself to use her professional detachment and skills to manage the situation. *Where have I heard those words so recently,* Natalie wondered. It was odd.

"Good, I'm keeping Monet!" she declared vehemently, without responding verbally.

Natalie decided she would leave Lisa alone for now, but not too long.

The question was what role would Lisa choose

to play? Natalie's friend or a jealous girlfriend. For the first time in my life, I can't trust the one person I thought would always be there for me. Natalie's heart ached with a sense of alienation, knowing she would not cause a rift within their shared childhood group of friends by forcing them to choose sides. They know both of us well enough to see the truth. This involves no one else, so I will keep it contained.

"It appears I am experiencing a state of different realities, with one foot in this life and another in multiple dimensions," she spoke out loud as Monet cocked her head to understand. Natalie implored to her cherished companion, "I know you won't leave me, and I vow I will never surrender you, either!"

As her mind whirled with disbelief, Natalie failed to take to heart the notifications of movement outside her door. Focused on seeing Ben, she readied herself to take off, forgetting there were two stalkers waiting for the ideal time.

Chapter 9

The deep blue 4-Runner sped towards the reservation, hugging the road's curves as if it was on a rail. Natalie's mind was reeling from what was taking place between herself and Lisa. "I've got someone stalking me and Lisa needs to act like a jealous schoolgirl without even speaking about it?" she ranted emphatically, impatient to get to Ben's home. Monet listened intuitively, understanding the energy behind the words.

A vivid awareness of foreboding filled Natalie's senses as a vision of a man flashed before her mind's eye. A fleeting impression of someone familiar driving a car caused her hair to stand on edge. Instinctively glancing into the rearview mirror, a glimpse of a car was far behind.

Looking back to the road, Natalie screamed and swerved as she over corrected to escape hitting a deer on the pavement directly ahead. Screeching tires preceded the crunch of metal as the car rolled over repeatedly before coming to its resting place, slamming against the trees bordering the parkway. A dark sedan that had been discreetly following pulled over behind them, alone in a remote area in the woods.

"Monet!" Natalie urgently cried out from the wreckage, eyes flickering as her head rolled around, consciousness moving in and out.

"She survived," a vaguely recognized male voice replied. "I know she is important to you, so I will bring her with us. Rest and I'll take care of you both."

Unable to open her eyes completely or remain awake, relief that Monet was being cared for allowed Natalie to sink back into the darkness. The driver pulled Natalie and Monet from the debris, secured them in his car, and sped away unseen before the crash site was discovered and reported.

Faint images materialized as Natalie awoke from unconsciousness in a room she did not recognize and a bed that was not her own. A squishy pillow cradled her aching head as a hazy recollection tried to emerge. "Why does my body feel like road kill and where the hell am

I?" she audibly whispered, failing to remember what had taken place. It's night-time, was her first deduction, noting the shadows cast by a night light in the strange bedroom. Instinctively, she attempted to sit up, but filled with horror to discover her ankle had a shackle around it and was secured to the metal bed frame. Her heart rate rocketed upon realizing she was a prisoner. Every fiber in her body froze as if it had plunged into an ice bath. Shuddering panic incapacitated her ability to think, breathe, or move as she wondered if she was having another nightmare. It's just as real as my past nightmares, she rationalized, and each one has been different and detailed. Clear thoughts were a struggle to put together as she battled between the emotions and a clouded sense of reality ravaging her judgment. This feels like coming out from under anesthesia. Her blurry thoughts cleared. Her tongue rolled around a parched mouth as she gratefully spotted a glass of water on a nightstand. Water has never tasted so good, she thought as it replenished her dry mouth and throat, finishing it with appreciation. Deep breaths and some rehydration enabled her thoughts to clear. *Well, now I've really got to pee. Let's examine what's been happening while I was dreaming.*

Steadying herself to come face to face with her captor, Natalie called out in a nervous voice.

"Hello! Can you help me?"

Footsteps sounded on a hardwood floor, making Natalie's stomach feel as though she was on a roller coaster. Slowly, the bedroom door creaked open. Natalie could feel tingling anticipation as her body shook with fear. The tingling accelerated to a sensation of being electrocuted, as shock coursed through her extremities, seeing Mr. Edward Bowden materialize from the shadows.

"Call me Ed," she could hear him say when he came in for his therapy sessions. Natalie found herself speechless as her mind attempted to comprehend that Mr. Bowden was in her nightmare. It was impossible to imagine this benign, browbeaten man could have a dark side to him, which eased her panic somewhat. Dreams are so strange; you never know who's going to show up or how they will behave, she observed, still feeling the ramifications of shock reverberating throughout her senses.

"Miss Edwards, I am so pleased that you are awake. Your car crash was quite nasty and I've been fearful about injuries. How do you feel?"

"Car crash?" Natalie repeated and asked simultaneously.

"Yes, I pulled you from the accident and brought you here!" he eagerly informed her.

Natalie felt like she was going through the black hole on Space Mountain before it plunged into the abyss, hanging on for her life as the unknown twists and turns knocked the breath from her lungs. Cloudy memories quickly gained clarity as the foreboding sensation she had felt right before the accident permeated her entirely. The image of a recognizable man driving a car flashed in her mind's eye once again. As she caught her breath, the recollection of a deer in the road made her muscles tighten as her body reflexively relived the car crash. The 4-Runner rolling over brought tears to her eyes as the force of an air bag exploding upon impact with the trees rendered her unconscious. I remember a familiar male voice telling me Monet was alive, and he will take care of us both. Natalie was astounded as she pictured Ed pulling her and Monet from the wreckage of the car and bringing them here, wherever here is. Suddenly, questions began forming in her mind faster than she could articulate. One thing was sure; this was no nightmare!

"I'm not in a dream?" she uttered as a statement more than a question.

"I'm sure it must feel like one, but the good news is you survived an awful crash and I'm taking care of you!"

Choosing to ignore the second part of Ed's statement for the moment, she desperately needed to know the answer to her next question. "How is Monet?" Dread filled her chest and time seemed to stop while awaiting his answer.

"Don't worry! I helped my father care for his animal patients when he was a veterinarian, so I knew what to do for her! The seatbelt harness she was wearing saved her life. Actually, the roll bars and air bags in your car probably saved you both! I suspect one of her front legs is broken. I have it in a splint and am giving her pain medication as well."

"I need to see her!" Panic rose as she pictured Monet in her car, rolling over and crashing into trees.

"Monet is sedated and should be left alone!" Ed sternly responded, becoming nervous.

The professional psychologist took over Natalie's irrationality, as she recognized the need to play along with a man whose psychological issues were obviously far worse than he had ever revealed in their counseling sessions. "I can already tell you've done so much for me, but I'm so worried! I'm concerned that Monet isn't fine, and you're just telling me she is to keep me calm. Can you please show me she is alive?" Natalie's lip quivered as she appealed to his ego.

Struggling with a decision, he finally relented as tears slid down Natalie's face and whimpers escaped for added benefit.

"She is in the kitchen. Can you make it that far?"

"Yes!" Natalie choked out through one last dramatic sob.

"I will return in a moment. I have to check on my mother first." Ed turned without waiting for a response and shut the door behind him as the click of a lock sounded.

Oh my God, I'm not IN a nightmare, my life has literally BECOME the nightmare! Her mind felt paralyzed with shock as adrenaline sped up a heart rate that was elevated to begin with. "You don't have time to lose your shit, Natalie! Think!" she sternly stated out loud. "If he wanted me dead, I would have been left on the side of the road or he could have killed me already. Since I'm shackled, he doesn't think I will stay here willingly." Reality hit her like a hard punch. "Ed is my stalker! He saved me from the car accident because he has been following me! How often has this guy followed me? I haven't noticed? No time to waste wondering. How do I survive this?"

Intuition gave her a game plan, and it would require acting skills and manipulation. He's got to think I am grateful to him for saving me and Monet, that he can trust me. I have got to stay in control and make him believe I'm a friend. Hastily, she gained control of her thoughts and put her plan into action.

"Oh my goodness, Ed, there you are!" she exclaimed with as much happiness and relief in her voice as she could feign when he returned. His shoulders eased with the belief Natalie was glad to see him and called him by his first name.

"Are you feeling well enough to move, Miss Edwards?"

Being as charming as she could muster under the circumstances, Natalie played the part of a grateful friend. Smiling sweetly, she implored, "Please call me Natalie! You saved my life, so that certainly changes the status of our relationship. Unfortunately, I truly don't know how I am doing without being able to get up and move around. I am bound to the bed," she nonchalantly motioned to the shackle around her ankle and continued to smile. "Would you be able to assist me to the bathroom before we see Monet and test how steady I am on my feet? My head is excruciating, but I really need to move around to check for injuries."

"Oh, I am truly sorry my mother put this on you," he lightly rested his hand on the shackle, his gaze lingering upon her leg as his fingers brushed her skin. "I'll have a talk with her again," he simply stated without further elaboration.

Resisting the urge to recoil or ask potentially inflammatory questions, Natalie replied, "Well, thank you, I would appreciate that. Might I go to the bathroom?"

"Of course. It's right down the hall. My bedroom is on the other side of the bathroom, so we'll have to share, but I cleaned it up for you," he answered, sounding eager to have her as a house guest.

"Oh! This is your house? That answers one of my questions."

"Well, as you know, I live with my mother so this is her house."

"Yes, is she here? I would love to meet her!" Natalie enthusiastically asked, attempting to gather information about her surroundings.

"Um, she is here, but is asleep. Her room is on the other side of the house. She won't be able to hear us, so you don't need to worry about disturbing her," he replied while removing a key from his pocket and unlocking the shackle.

She held her arms up as if waiting for him to assist her weight, knowing her body ached, but unable to determine if she was injured in her current state of shock. Ed bent down to her bed, allowing her to place her hands on his shoulders as he assisted her to a standing position. Instantly, the room spun. Her legs gave out, and he completely supported her body.

Natalie cried out in pain, but also in terror upon realizing she wasn't strong enough to fight her captor. Relenting to the understanding she would have to play her game with him for a while until she recovered more made her cry, but she let Ed believe it was all because of her physical state.

"Your pain medication has worn off. You can wait to move until I give you another dose and it kicks in if you prefer."

"You gave me pain meds? Um, how thoughtful," she added, trying to keep up her ruse. "How did you have some?"

Still holding her up so her head could acclimate to being in a standing position, Ed answered, "I don't think I told you during our sessions that my father was a veterinarian and still practiced until he died last year. His office is filled with medications and equipment. Did you know animals require many of the same medications as humans do?"

"How convenient," Natalie murmured. "Okay, I think I'm ready to walk. Can we aim for the bathroom?" She loathed having to touch Ed, but needed him to believe she couldn't physically escape. Suspicion that pain killers were not the only drugs he had given her nagged at the back of her mind as she remained in a semi-delirious state, feeling as though she was underwater.

A slow walk to the bathroom gave her time to scan what little she could see from the hallway. A barely lit living room was at the end of the hall, just past the door on the other side of the bathroom, which she assumed was Ed's bedroom.

"I think I'm okay to go in by myself if you can get me to the counter."

"I'll be right outside if you need anything. Just call out!"

Natalie gave what she hoped appeared to be a grateful smile as he closed the door behind her. Then she heard a click. A deadbolt on the outside secured her in the bathroom, just like the bedroom. Anger overrode fear as she perceived he had planned on bringing a captive to this house, whether it was her or someone else. "You little son of a bitch," she whispered out loud. The doorknob still had its own lock on it, she turned it out of spite. Bars on the window behind the home made curtain made for a dead end. Well, I won't be escaping from the bathroom. Let's see how big a mess my face is. After using the toilet, she washed her hands while examining her reflection in the mirror of the medicine cabinet hanging over the small sink. Yellowed linoleum slightly adhered to her bare feet, sticky from too much pine sol that heavily scented the room. Slight burns on her face stung from where the air bag had deployed and minor cuts on her arms from glass appeared to have been cleaned. An almost unbearable pain in her neck going up into her skull indicated whiplash. Aside from those minor details, Natalie was incredulous that she had no other serious injuries, just severe soreness. Looking up to the Heavens, she whispered a prayer of thanks for the protection and prayed for one request, "Please get me and Monet out of here alive!"

"I'm ready," Natalie called out after turning the old lock on the doorknob. Able to manage fine on her own after the chance to stand for a while, she pretended to need help as Ed entered.

One arm wrapped around Ed's waist for support, Natalie rested her free hand on his chest and let her eyes tear up as she looked pitifully into his, playing the part of a damsel in distress.

The slow trek to the kitchen revealed plenty of detail about the dated house that felt more like a museum. The living room was dusty and untouched, while the kitchen was obviously used. In the corner, laying on a blanket, was Monet. Her right front paw had a splint. She panted, and the sedative prevented her from acknowledging her beloved friend.

Natalie's hand flew to her mouth, "Oh my God!"

"She's okay. She's sleeping and we shouldn't upset her."

"I just want to touch Monet! I promise not to bother her!" Natalie delicately made her way to the blanket, using the Formica counter for feigned support as she leaned over and caressed Monet's mane. *I'm fine and we are going to escape,* Natalie telepathically communicated, unsure if Monet would hear. Unexpectedly, light brown eyes opened and Monet's tail thumped weakly against the linoleum. Natalie smiled for her one minor victory, her heart fortified knowing Monet saw and heard her, which would give her protector strength as well.

Ed stood directly behind Natalie and forcefully guided her away.

"Thank you," she somberly stated, truly meaning the words. "Can I help you make something for dinner?" Natalie volunteered, hoping to avoid being shackled to the bed.

"Actually, I have a surprise if you're hungry! But you must go lay back down. I let you see your dog. Now it's time to rest." Ed's demeanor indicated he was not to be pushed any further.

"Of course, you're right," she complied, not wanting to push her luck or arouse suspicion.

Settled back in the bed, Ed went to place the shackle around Natalie's ankle again. "Ed, is that necessary? I thought we were friends!"

"It's for your safety," he answered without looking directly at her. "I'll be right back with your surprise."

A familiar aroma announced Ed's return as he opened her bedroom door, holding a plate and a glass of wine. "Surprise!" He beamed, proud of himself as her dinner and cocktail was placed on the nightstand.

Truly as stunned as she appeared, Natalie's eyes widened at the sight of P.F. Chang's Mongolian Beef steaming on the plate. There had been little time for her to fully process the fact Ed had trailed every movement she had made and knew more about her than she cared to acknowledge. Images flashed through her mind as she remembered an energy watching when she stood in her apartment window, the shadowed figure on the running path, a dark sedan speeding away from the parking lot when Monet chased someone, and the empty elevator at her apartment when an unidentified person ducked around the corner to escape being sighted. Staring blankly at her dinner, the last session with Ed jolted her memory of a Starbucks latte made with almond milk.

"I certainly surprised you, didn't I?" Ed grinned, misinterpreting Natalie's silence as overwhelmed joy.

Snapping out of her trance, Natalie quickly recovered. "Oh, you have no idea!" she truthfully answered, hoping sarcasm wasn't detected. "I bet this is my favorite wine, too!" she tentatively smiled. "You keep surprising me!"

"I'll let you enjoy your dinner," he smiled to himself as he unlocked the shackle and hastily retreated, leaving Natalie no time to react.

Natalie returned the smile as genuinely as she could manage. "Thank you, Ed. You really are something else."

Ed waved sheepishly as he closed the bedroom door behind him. Click went another lock from the outside, just like the bathroom door.

Chapter 10

Head pounding, Natalie winced as sunlight emanated from around the draperies. She gripped her temples with both palms; she struggled to relax her muscles, noting how clenched they were. It's preposterous to unwind when you're a prisoner. Forcing herself to sit up, she spotted a note on the nightstand and the shackle secured around her ankle again. Her head shook in disbelief. "I was counting on waking up from this nightmare," she lamented.

"I've left you ibuprofen if you desire it while I am gone. I won't be long." Her dinner plate and wine glass removed and replaced with water.

"So fucking thoughtful, Ed," she muttered as she swallowed the pills. "Thanks for poisoning my dinner, asshole."

Footsteps on the worn hardwood alerted Natalie before the bedroom door opened. A wiry yet sturdy looking elderly woman stood in the doorway with a pistol pointed at Natalie.

"He got hisself another whore, I see!" She yelled, jabbing the gun in Natalie's direction.

Stunned, Natalie stammered, "You must be Mrs. Bowden! I'm Natalie Edwards! I'm Ed's psychologist and he's keeping me against my will! Can you please help me?"

"Yew purty gals keep puttin' spells on my youngster, actin' like yew done nuttin' wrong! Well, this is what yew git!" the deranged old woman spat as she steadied the weapon, preparing to fire.

Natalie threw herself from the bed, her left ankle still confined, with her body settling on the floor. A chain enabled her foot some room for movement. She hollered for help, realizing it was pointless as she hit the ground hard, the bullet striking the wall behind the spot where she had been sitting.

"Mother! NO!" Ed's irate yet frantic voice sounded. "You cannot murder another one! I love her!" he scolded and professed, yanking the gun from her grip as he reached the bedroom just in time.

"She ain't good 'nuff fer yew! Just like them other

ones! I shackled her up, but yew stole my key! Yer too soft, trustin' people! I gotta put a bullet in her so she won't escape an' so yew won't git hurt!" the crazed woman howled.

"Natalie is a psychologist, mother! She speaks to me and understands me!"

Her tone became deeper as she narrowed her eyes. The demented woman scowled at Ed and warned, "She's a witch an' cast a spell on yew! Now, give me my gun back an' git outta here! I gotta save yew, son. Ain't nobody luv yew like yer momma can," she crossed over from menacing to cajoling as she stroked the side of Ed's face with her withered hand.

Falling under his mother's own spell, Ed reached up and placed his hand over hers as it rested possessively on his face. "I love you, mama, but I won't let you kill her. We can talk about this later."

Mrs. Bowden directed a menacing glare towards Natalie, as she hissed in her direction. "I ain't done with yew, missy! That ain't my only gun!" she threatened and retreated down the hall, muttering under her breath.

Natalie's neck and elbow hurt from the strain of reinforcing her body while straining to witness the scene of nearly losing her life. As she lowered herself down onto the stale carpet, her left foot remained twisted, dangling from the chain and shackle. "You can't make this shit up," she vocalized out loud in a state of shock, eyes wide with disbelief.

Ed rushed to her aide. "Here, let me help you up!" he proclaimed as he worriedly assisted Natalie from the floor and back onto the bed without unlocking the iron.

You can flip your shit later, she silently counseled herself. He trusts me slightly, so let's help him see the truth of this distorted relationship he has with his mother. Maybe that's how I survive. It's time for a therapy session, Natalie assessed as her professional persona took over.

"Ed, can you please have a seat in the chair," Natalie asked, using her counselor tone of voice.

He obediently perched himself on the edge of a chair near the door. "I'm so sorry, Miss, uh… Natalie! My mother was asleep when I left to get some groceries. I assumed you would be safe! I really should get them out of the car."

"The groceries will be alright for now. We need to chat about your mother," she counseled, sitting on her hands to control them from shaking and struggling to keep a tremor from her voice. "Ed, I'm not the first woman to be here and it sounds as though the previous, um… guests did not leave alive."

Ed's eyes cast down as he wrung his hands.

"I am deeply touched by how much you care for me. Did you care for the other women as well?"

"Oh, yes! Very much!" He sincerely emphasized. "We were to be together forever. I still miss things about both of them." He confessed, looking dreamily into the distance.

"Let's think through how the pattern of behavior is repeating, just like we've talked about before in our sessions. Other female 'friends' of yours were here. Where are they?"

Ed buried his head in his hands and, swaying back and forth, he sobbed.

"Ed, please look at me," Natalie encouraged gently, yet firmly. "Did your mother kill them? It is imperative that we face the truth of this situation."

Tears streamed from his eyes as he nodded an affirmation to her question.

"How many were there and where are they?" She inquired, fighting for control over her panic.

"There were two others," he sniveled, striving to maintain himself under control as well. "Mother shot my girlfriends while I was out!" He broke down with shuddering shoulders and raspy gasps for air. "Sometimes if I kept the shackle on, Mother would leave them alone for a time. She didn't like either of the women; said they weren't suitable enough for me, but I loved them!" he implored.

"How did you feel when you found them dead?" she urged, wanting him to relive the horror in hopes he would try to avert having a repeat performance with her.

Ed sucked in his breath as he wailed harder and his body quivered, envisioning their sightless eyes and lifeless bodies. "I was so sad it hurt!" He choked through sobs. "Burying their bodies in the woods was the worst thing I've ever had to do! I made nice grave stones by planting flowers." The crying subsided at the memory of the blooming flowers. "I didn't want them to die." He finished with a few remaining hiccups.

"Why do you think it will end differently with me, Ed? What did you just stop your mother from doing?"

"Killing you," he responded, eyes glaring straight ahead he continued to shudder and nervously hiccup.

"Yes, and if you hadn't gotten home when you did, you be digging a grave for me too." She turned and pointed to the bullet hole in the wall behind her. "Ed, I care very much for you, too, but we need to get out of here- together." She emphasized the last word, knowing there was a stronger chance of convincing Ed to escape with her as opposed to letting her go.

His eyes snapped to attention as he grasped the significance of her words. "And leave mother?" He worried.

"Have you ever heard the saying by Albert Einstein, 'The definition of insanity is doing the same thing over and over again, and expecting a different result?' You just stopped your mother from murdering me." Her voice caught in her throat, abandoning her calm façade.

"It's a matter of time before she does and you know that!" Reality rapidly gripped her senses as she pictured herself shot to death in the bed, with panic threatening to overcome her sensibility. "You must cease repeating your behavior!" Natalie implored with authority, with a hint of an underlying caring sentiment. "We can make sure they get care for your mother. She needs help, Ed. People who kill others are not well. It must be miserable for her trying to maintain control over you to the point of murder, and you're clearly upset to lose the women you love. Let's do something and make this situation better." Natalie prayed her rationale made sense to Ed and provided him with hope and an option that would enable her to live.

Nodding his head with a serious expression on his face, he eventually spoke. "I'll think about what you've said. For now, I need to prepare us some breakfast."

Natalie's heart sank as she realized she believed he would take action promptly. "Okay, that's fair. Please don't take too long, though. I want us both to have a future to look forward to." She encouraged without lying by leaving out the word together. "First, may I please go to the bathroom?"

Ed held the gun by his side as he supervised Natalie's movements. His demeanor remained somber, so she played the part of an obedient prisoner. Her intuition told her he did not know which way he was leaning towards; to help or kill her. Besides, she needed him to continue taking care of Monet, who he allowed her to see again briefly. A much needed hot shower was permitted. Natalie relished the feel of the water as it relaxed her sore body and cleared her mind. "Thank you for a hot shower." She whispered, fervently hoping it wasn't her last. Ed had set out fresh clothes for her and she hesitated, wondering about their origin; did they belong to a former captive or did he buy them for her? There was no one's energy attached to them she could detect, so she decided they were new. They didn't look worn, anyway. An eerie sensation of being watched urged her to dress quickly. Fearing for her life, every second made her feel as though she were living in a haunted mansion. Constantly afraid that something would lash out from nowhere and "get" her. Childhood nightmares come to life, she reflected.

Natalie sat shackled to the bed, struggling to connect with the energies of the two women who had occupied the room before her. Without painkillers or drugs in her system, her intuition was sharp and she could detect a presence. A thick book lying next to her on the bed flipped open of its own volition while the click on the door lock turned. A current of needles passed through her body as she reacted to the book and simultaneously envisioned Mrs. Bowden aiming a pistol at her.

Snatching the hardback and raising it in the air as a projectile, she reinforced her body, preparing to jump from the bed again. Ed slowly opened the door, announcing brunch. Natalie released her breath as she exhaled in tremendous relief. The smell of food normally would make Natalie's stomach growl, but she had no appetite. He saw the terror in her eyes as she lowered the book. Ed's somber mood intensified as he realized the reason for Natalie's fear.

"I won't let her harm you." he reassured.

"I'm certain you mean that, Ed, but you can't stop her, remember? There are two dead women and I'm going to be next. Did you know their energies are still trapped here? We have got to do something! Please," she pleaded.

Ed ignored her attempt at conversation, set down the plate of food on the nightstand with a cup of coffee and unlocked the shackle. "You should at least enjoy eating without that on."

Carefully choosing her words, but determined to get through to Ed, Natalie asked, "Is there anything in my meal that will make me tired? It is important that I am conscious in case I need to defend myself."

Quickly exiting the room, Ed's movement abruptly halted as he comprehended the implication of her words. "No, and I'll leave the shackle off. I know something has to change. And I'm sorry the other women are stuck here. They don't deserve to be in Purgatory," he responded without making eye contact as he locked the door behind him.

Chapter 11

It was a relief to move around without being chained to the bed. Natalie stretched, did sit-ups and push-ups, squats and lunges despite her sore body. A soft knock at the door made her jump.

"It's me, Ed," she heard.

"Uh, come in." Natalie said, confused about the sudden change in protocol.

Ed remained in the doorway, watchful that Natalie might attempt to escape. "I thought I should let you know it's me at the door, so you won't be frightened."

Thinking back to when he arrived at her room with brunch, she recalled having a book ready to throw, in case it was his mother coming to kill her again. "I appreciate your kindness," she smiled.

"I don't know what to do. I should have never

taken you here, but I love you!" he blurted out, with eyes cast down.

"Ed, can you come in the room so we won't be overheard? I'll sit on the bed and you can sit in the chair again." She responded as hope rose in her chest that he would help her.

He took a moment to decide, but came in and sat down, resting the pistol he had taken from his mother in his lap. "I don't know where the other gun is, but at least I've kept this one from her," he explained, as she eyed the weapon.

Scenarios raced through Natalie's mind about how she could escape in the moment with the shackle off. Monet was her first concern, and she couldn't risk the life of her protector if Ed would listen to reason. Natalie felt she owed it to herself and Monet to find out, so she sat on the bed as promised. Besides, the chair was near the door and she wouldn't be able to make it past him.

"I need to understand why all of this happened so I can support you, Ed, and we can determine what we should do," she began, mindful to include them both in the plan. "Where did you get the notion that the women you love need to be held captive?"

Ed looked away, averting his eyes, but responded. "When I was young, I went to my father's office out back to see if I could help. He had forgotten to lock the door, so when I went in, I saw a woman. She was roped to a chair with a bandana tied around her mouth. My dad's back was to me, but I could see he had no clothes on. I knew little then, but I knew enough that I didn't want to see anything else."

"How did you feel when you witnessed that scene? It seems like it's still a vivid memory, so it must have made an enormous impact."

"It's like it just happened!" he responded, excited Natalie grasped its importance. Eager to unburden his emotions, he continued. "Of course, I was shocked! It scared me he would see me, but it was also exciting! Part of me wanted to keep watching to see what happened, but I knew he would punish me." Ed's eyes stared past Natalie as he recalled his first impression of a relationship; excitement barely contained as if he were recalling a baseball game.

Natalie's emotions warred within her between outrage, pity, and disgust. As a professional psychologist, she learned to disregard and put aside her personal opinion while counseling, but treating a patient who had kidnapped her and put her life in jeopardy made following professional protocol challenging.

"Did you talk to your father about it?" she asked in

a neutral tone.

Ed squirmed in his chair. "Yes, I asked who tied her up in his office. He looked scared, but told me they were in love and not to tell mother because it would hurt her feelings. I knew he was afraid Mother would find out." An angry expression crossed Ed's face as he went on. "I got mad because I knew it wasn't fair to mother for him to love someone else."

"But, Ed, he tied the woman up! Didn't that worry you or make you think maybe your father was doing something wrong?" Natalie's voice rose as she attempted to contain her temper.

Ed's eyes flashed to hers, hardened and devoid of emotion. "There were always women tied up on TV," he emphasized with a note of defiance. "Whenever dad's office door was locked, I'd peek through the blinds and see women tied up with him. He loved a lot of women!" he defended.

"Ed," she began, forcing composure and neutrality into her voice, "What you saw on TV and witnessed by your father was not love. It was abuse and persecution. I can see by your body language you realize that's the truth and you know the difference!"

His defensiveness ceased as shame crept across his face and settled into his body, slumping in the chair while gawking at a stain on the carpet.

"The excitement is intoxicating to you, isn't it?" Natalie asked, her voice clear of judgment, making a clinical observation and assessment.

Ed's head snapped up, realization overwhelmed him as his mouth hung ajar and eyes reflected comprehension of Natalie's statement.

Natalie's heart almost felt for young Ed, empathizing with what it was like to be humiliated without understanding what was wrong. "Is the adventure worth killing me for? What do you guess happened to your father's lovers, Ed?" She shook her head and raised her eyebrows for emphasis. "He couldn't let them go free…" She let the sentence hang for dramatic effect.

Ed's eyes filled with horror as it forced him to contemplate something his mind always knew, but he had never faced. He gripped his skull with his hands, shaking his head. "This is too much! I wouldn't have hurt them!"

"Did your mother ever find out?"

Ed's hands went from his head to covering his mouth. His eyes closed as he attempted to block the memories. He began swaying backward and forth in the armchair like he had during their last "session".

Natalie instinctively realized what had happened,

but needed him to articulate it himself.

"What did she do when she found out?"

"She shot them!" he squealed, standing up, face red and full of rage as the pistol thudded on the floor, falling from his lap. He moved closer to the door to escape this questioning. It was too much to handle.

"Did they deserve to be killed?" She honed in on his buried emotions.

"Yes!" he yelled with passion. "No!" he relented with truthful realization. "They weren't there by choice, just like you!" His body leaned against the door and slid down to the floor, where he sat hugging his knees. "Oh my God, what have I done? What kind of monster am I?" he lamented, glancing to the heavens for answers. "My parents are monsters and so am I!" Devastation reverberated in his cry.

"You were both emotionally abused, Ed." Natalie tried to placate him, knowing it was a truthful statement. "She reacted from a state of trauma. Now that trauma repeats for her when you bring home captive women. Your mother will continue to kill us because that's the only coping mechanism she knows. End this cycle NOW, Ed. Let me live!"

He remained seated on the floor, staring blankly

ahead, contemplating the new childhood realizations and the present situation. Finally, he spoke. "Will mother and I go to jail?"

"As your psychologist, I would advocate for psychiatric treatment instead. You did not kill anyone, so that increases your odds. Your mother will not pass a mental health exam. She would be…"

"Locked up in an insane asylum," he interrupted, concerned.

"Taken care of in a mental hospital," Natalie gently closed the sentence, hope filling her so intently she could barely sit still.

"Will you come visit me?" he asked with a catch in his voice.

"I don't know what is allowed, but if I can, yes, I will come see you," she truthfully explained.

"I don't have anywhere to run. I couldn't take care of mother. This is my only option," he deduced, feeling defeated.

"Thank you for caring for me enough to work this out, Ed." Natalie genuinely expressed.

"Mother will kill you if I don't do something and I can't bear the thought of that, especially now that I realize the truth. I would be guilty of murder because now I know better. I just wanted someone to love." he confessed, his heart feeling as though someone had ripped it from his chest and replaced with uncertain fear. "I'll drive you home or to a hospital; wherever you choose to go." He rose, shifted around, and opened the door.

Standing on the opposite side was Mrs. Bowden, eavesdropping on their conversation. True to her word, she raised her spare pistol, focusing on Natalie.

"Yew ain't gonna take me or my son, yew connivin' hussy!" She squealed as she fired a shot.

Ed deflected her hand, causing the bullet to miss Natalie. "Mother, this ends now! No more killing! You need help!"

The two grappled for the gun, Mrs. Bowden exhibiting surprising strength for an elderly woman.

"Mother, please don't do this!"

Natalie had leapt from the bed and was in a fetal position in the room's corner, arms covering her head, praying Ed was successful in wrangling the gun from the demented old woman. The sounds of a struggle abruptly ceased as another shot fired.

"Aaahhhh, my boy! Look what yew made me do!" Manic rage and devastation consumed the irrational shrew.

Natalie's head whipped up to learn what had taken place. Ed lay at the foot of the bed with a bullet wound to his chest. His eyes were still open with a stunned expression. Shocked and frozen, Natalie's mind refused to accept what her eyes were witnessing.

Mrs. Bowden was seething as she stood over her son. A look of contempt replaced grief as she raised the pistol once more. "I hope yew go ta hell for this!" If she were a hound, she would froth at the mouth for certain.

Before she could take aim, Natalie heard a growl as Monet sank her teeth deep into Mrs. Bowden's calf, shaking her head, tearing muscle and tissue. Piercing screams filled the air as the old woman went down to the ground. Blood oozing down her leg, she snatched one of Ed's shirts, found on the floor nearby to stop the bleeding. The graceful white shepherd now had bloodstains on her pristine coat of fur. I could not blame her. She was defending me.

Natalie's adrenaline helped her spring like a cat from her huddled position. The injured mother pointed the pistol at Monet, virtually face to face with the shepherd. Natalie's foot brushed against Ed's gun, lying next to him. Without a conscious thought, she scooped it up and pulled the trigger, overriding the safety. Time passed in slow motion. In this moment, she had no sympathy. Natalie swore she could see the bullet leave the chamber and travel through the air, striking Mrs. Bowden in the neck. Her body went limp as her weapon dropped to the ground with a hard thud. What had she done? Natalie tossed the pistol she used to the corner of the room where she had crouched, unconsciously horrified. She had just shot someone, self-defense or not she did not know what her fate would be. Adrenaline numbed Natalie's emotions as she rushed to inspect Monet, who whined and wagged her tail furiously at the sight of her beloved friend.

"Oh my God, you saved my life, you beautiful Angel!" hugging her close.

A quick inspection showed no additional injury to the heroic pooch, so Natalie turned her urgent attention to Ed.

"Ed!" she frantically pleaded, "Please be alive! Squeeze my hand if you can hear me!"

His eyes had closed, but she could detect a pulse and see that he was breathing, although labored. Holding his hand, she felt a slight pressure as he tried to squeeze hers.

"Oh, dear God, thank you!" she prayed.

Patting his pockets, she found his cell phone and called 911.

"I don't know the address!" She panicked, conveying

to the operator. "It's the house of Edward Bowden, but I'm sure it's in his parent's name! His father was a veterinarian, and that's all I know! My name is Natalie Edwards, and I have been captive here for two days! I'm uninjured, but Ed is severely wounded and I don't know about his mother! Please help me!" She lost her composure.

Instructions to put pressure on Ed's wound helped her mind focus as she ran into the bathroom to grab towels, stepping over Mrs. Bowden without looking.

After what seemed an eternity, sirens approached the house. Natalie could hear pounding at the front door. She called out for help. The sound of the front door splintered as a batting ram was used, brought relief that help was seconds away.

"We're in here!"

Police and paramedics ran down the hall, stopping short at Monet, who had laid down, tired from her broken front leg and exertion.

"I think the woman is dead and Ed is still alive, but barely!" Natalie assessed.

Paramedics made their way into the bedroom, while officers moved Monet with ease.

Mrs. Bowden was pronounced dead at the scene. Ed was quickly rushed to the hospital and placed under police custody. Natalie requested an officer drive her and Monet to the Veterinarian. Only after the shepherd had been treated was she willing to be taken to the hospital for her own evaluation.

Chapter 12

The stark hospital room felt cramped with police officers and FBI agents vying for answers from Natalie, who was in a state of shock. Bright light stung her eyes and added to an excruciating headache caused by a concussion and whiplash from the car accident. Natalie refused pain medication, fearful of feeling drugged like she had been while in captivity. PTSD was a sign she recognized in herself and knew therapy was on the horizon. For now, dealing with the chaos of being injured in an accident, kidnapped, and then almost murdered left her feeling vulnerable. Normally, her best friend would be there for support, but Lisa was nowhere to be seen and Natalie didn't know if her friend knew or cared. The doctor came in to update her on test results and became irritated his patient wasn't being given a chance to rest, so ordered everyone out.

"Your mother and brother are on their way," he reassured. "You have them listed as emergency contacts," he explained upon seeing Natalie's confused expression.

"Oh my goodness, of course. But I'm okay and there's no longer an emergency," she argued, not looking forward to facing her mother, with whom she had rare contact. Natalie had been meaning to call her brother, but always made the excuse of not wanting to bother him. They stationed him at Cherry Point as part of the 2nd Marine Aircraft Wing and Fleet Readiness Center. Natalie never knew when he was on a mission and was often afraid to find out.

"The police contacted them when they found your car," Dr. Moore explained. "They located your phone at the scene of the accident and have been in contact with your mom and brother, trying to locate you. You were nowhere to be found."

"That makes sense. Do you know where my phone is?" Natalie hopefully inquired.

"I know they put some of your belongings in a bag," he responded, looking around for the standard plastic hospital bag. "Ah, here it is!" He handed the phone to Natalie after locating the bag in a corner and fishing it out.

"Oh wow! My phone looks as banged up as I am!" she observed, noting the cracked screen. "But just like me, it still works!" Scrolling through, she noted several frantic texts from her tribe of friends and quickly drafted a group response, including Lisa. Next, she texted her mother and brother, telling them she was fine, there was no need to come, and she would call them later.

"Too late, we're already here," a familiar male voice sounded from the doorway.

Natalie's heart caught in her throat with joy at the sight of her brother, Andrew, and a genuine smile lit up her face for the first time in a long while.

Two giant strides from his tall, muscular frame had him standing next to the bed, giving her a bear hug. "Oh geez, are you hurt?" he panicked, releasing Natalie and looking her over for injuries.

"I'm sore, but other than a concussion and whiplash, I think I'll live. Am I right Dr. Moore?"

"I was just about to fill you in on your results. Yes, you are correct. I do not know how you basically walked away from a rollover. You must have angels working overtime!"

"Oh, I do! And we all need a vacation!"

"I'll write you a script for that along with physical

therapy for your neck injury," the doctor joked. "I'll give you some time with your family now. Send one of them out to let the police know when they can come in and talk to you," he said, shaking hands with Andrew and patting Natalie's mother on the shoulder as he passed her in the doorway.

"Hello, mom," Natalie called as her mother stood tentatively just outside the room. Andrew extended his arm, motioning for her to enter.

Tears streaming down her face, Louise gently sat on the side of the bed and reached her hand out to stroke Natalie's hair. "We've been frantic, worrying about you."

The relief Natalie felt to have her family there allowed her to lose her stoic composure as she cried. "I didn't know if I was going to make it," she choked through tears, as her mother pulled Natalie close and held her. It released decades of stored emotions. Perhaps my angels are helping to resolve so many past issues, she thought.

Andrew swiped tears off his face. The thought of losing his big sister was far more traumatic than any mission he felt. He sat on the opposite side of the bed and put his enormous arms around the two of them, creating a family huddle.

Pent-up emotions boiled over for Natalie as she sobbed uncontrollably, letting the fear flow from her in the safety of her mother and brother's arms. It had been so long that she carried her burdens alone. It felt good to free them and be supported. Knowing what she must do, she steadied herself after her cry.

Natalie sent her brother out to bring in the police and FBI so she could recant the entire story once, instead of having to relive it multiple times. Andrew's jaw and fists remained clenched, while his brilliant blue eyes hardened with fury as he listened to his sister's story. Louise lost all color in her face and held on to the arms of the chair for support, envisioning Natalie's words.

"Is this guy, Ed, here in this hospital?" Andrew sharply asked the lead police investigator.

"Yes, but he's in custody and has an officer in the room," the investigator pointedly replied, tracking Andrew's thoughts of taking matters into his own hands. "He's not about to go free. Ever. Let us take care of Mr. Bowden." He met everyone's eyes and waited for their affirmation.

"There's one more thing we need to be clear on," her protective brother declared.

"Natalie shot the whacko mother in self-defense. Is she going to be charged for a crime?"

Natalie's head spun from the image of Ed's mother,

lying lifeless on the floor amidst a pool of blood. "Oh God, I'm going to be sick!" she blurted, scrambling to reach the bedpan before emptying the contents of her stomach into it.

A nurse rushed to clean up the mess and gave Natalie a sympathetic glance.

"We have a complete deposition from Mr. Bowden attesting to the necessity of Ms. Edward's actions. He also disclosed the murders of two other women by his mother and the locations of their bodies. There will be no charges filed against Ms. Edwards," the Detective firmly stated. Relief flooded the small hospital room, replacing apprehension.

Law enforcement finished getting Natalie's statement, asked an endless number of questions, and finally wrapped things up for the time being. By that time, the hospital discharge papers were ready, and Natalie was free to go home.

"Would you consider staying with me for a while?" Louise asked hopefully. "Andrew is there and it would be so nice for us all to be together."

It had been forever since the three of them had been together, and it surprised Natalie that the idea actually appealed to her. Without acknowledgement from her mother about her father's abusive behavior and its effects on the family, Natalie had distanced herself, instead of continually reliving the trauma with each encounter. Until this moment, she didn't realize how much she still needed and missed her mother.

"That actually sounds nice, mom. Thank you," she accepted with tenderness in her voice. "I'll have to get Monet from the vet tomorrow, though. We're a team now!"

"Oh, it will be wonderful to have a dog in the house! Your father would never allow one."

"Technically, Monet is Lisa's dog, but that is another story. I'll tell you about it over a bottle of wine!"

"Now you're talking my language!" Andrew chimed in.

"Oh, and I'll need to bring Sage when we stop by my apartment! She must be so lonely without me the past two days!"

"She's so pretty, I might not give her back," Louise teased.

Everyone's spirits lifted with the anticipation of being together again.

Numb from aftershock and a false sense of security, Natalie failed to sense the eyes intently watching her every move as she left the hospital.

Chapter 13

"You knew someone was stalking you and didn't fucking tell me?" Andrew was irate with concern and didn't care who knew it as they strolled around their old neighborhood.

"It wasn't anything I could prove; just a series of circumstantial happenings and my intuition giving me messages and warnings. I can't call you every time I get a terrible sense about something!"

"Yes! Yes, you can!" he argued. "Not everyone is a psychic medium and is in tune with everything going on around them! If YOU think something's wrong, then it IS!"

"But there was nothing I could DO!" Natalie argued back. "Trust me, Lisa and I and the gang went through all the options together and had a plan in place."

"And how did that work out for ya?" He

sarcastically quipped.

Natalie didn't have a good argument for Andrew's last point. "What would you have done if I had told you?" she challenged.

"I would have had you come stay on base with me where he couldn't get through security!"

"What about my job? I couldn't have driven six hours back and forth every day!"

"Then I would have come to you!"

"Oh yeah, I've got a big picture of that! 'I'm sorry Commander, but my big sister needs me to stay with her for a while. She's a psychic medium and thinks someone is watching her," Natalie mocked. "We've both got busy, important lives and couldn't have done anything differently!"

"We'll never know, will we?"

"We are taking a walk while mom cooks dinner to relax, not to argue. This is pointless now. Can we please let it go? I'm safe and I'd like to focus on recovering emotionally and physically."

"Fine, but never keep me in the dark again–please. I can't imagine what you've been through, but mom and I have been in our own hell worrying about you. I never want to feel like that again. I couldn't forgive myself if something happened to you I could have prevented."

Guilt flooded her rationalizations. Ben believed she had two stalkers, but she hadn't told her brother. The police had arrested one and was in custody. If Ben was right, then one more was still out there. A chill ran up her spine and she visibly shook in response to that thought.

"What?!" Andrew reacted to her distress, fearing she was keeping something from him.

Choosing not to say anything yet about a second stalker, Natalie played it off as a traumatic response.

"I'm just really shaken by what happened. This is going to take effort to overcome and I'm in a state of shock right now. Don't worry, this is what I do for a living and I will absolutely take care of myself mentally AND physically." She wrapped her arms around his strong right arm as they strolled. I've been so consumed with Ed, I don't even know about a second stalker, she thought to herself. What if there isn't one or what if Ben was seeing Ed and misinterpreted his vision? I won't know for sure until I've had time without Mr. Bowden stalking me anymore to determine if there's someone else. I'm not about to be some paranoid female afraid of my shadow.

"I know you'll take care of yourself, but I'd appreciate it if you'd let me be there to help. I can take leave."

"Thanks, little Bro," she smiled and stood on her tippy toes to rub his cropped dark hair. There was no mistaking they were brother and sister from their appearance. "Let's see how I'm doing first before you put in for leave. I'd like to get back to a routine sooner than later. It will make me appear more normal and less like a victim, you know?"

"Yeah, I get it. Can't say I'd be any different. Hey, something just popped into my mind!"

Andrew never outright acknowledged the fact he possessed gifts like his sister's. Being in the military made him too macho to admit it. "They have created a new position for a shrink on base. They would station you at Cherry Point, but would also accompany some missions for immediate psychological desensitization. The job lasts for six months to give the military a chance to determine if it's beneficial. You interested?"

Natalie stopped walking and stared at her brother with genuine contemplation. "Seriously?!" she exclaimed.

"Yeah, it could be a wonderful change. The best part is you would be close so I can keep an eye on you!" He looked around as though scoping out the surroundings, not realizing how accurate his feigned protectiveness was. "For real, it might be an interesting next step for you and it would give you a chance to leave behind some traumatic shit for a while. Since you're my sister, maybe I can get you in without too much red tape."

They began walking again as Natalie pondered the idea. "I can't believe I'm saying this, but I love the idea! Look, I've got chills all over!" she excitedly observed, holding her arms out to show him the goose bumps. Chills were her way of recognizing her body's sign that something resonated with her soul purpose.

"Sweet! I'll give my Commanding Officer a buzz tomorrow! Not to change the subject, but something is bugging me. Where's Lisa? She's practically my sister, too, and I haven't heard from her."

"That's bugging me as well. We had a falling out, but given the severity of what happened to me, I thought for sure she would have texted or called. I sent out a group text and everyone responded except her. I don't know if she's still mad or what. I'll ask the gang if anyone has heard from her." Andrew was close with their childhood friends as well, including Lisa, even though he was a year younger.

"Why do you have her dog?"

"She let Monet stay with me for protection, but when we had our 'altercation', Lisa took her back. The next day, Monet ran across town and came back to me."

"Ouch, that had to have stung." He winced, knowing if Natalie wanted to elaborate, she would.

"Yeah. The accident and kidnapping happened the same day, so I haven't had the opportunity to make amends." Natalie almost choked on the word kidnapping. It still felt like one of her nightmares and seemed surreal that it actually happened.

Natalie's intuition was bothering her about Lisa. She contributed it to their strained relationship because of Jared. Her stomach lurched at the thought of him, but she was too exhausted to give her energy to it.

"Let's drink wine," she suggested as they headed up the driveway.

"You're reading my mind," Andrew smiled, wrapping his arm around her shoulders and giving his big sister a sideways hug.

Her brother had always behaved as though he was the older sibling; protecting Natalie and taking on responsibilities within the family. Aside from Lisa, Andrew had been Natalie's confidant and friend growing up. After they both left for college, they discovered they could sense each other's feelings and thoughts. The connection faded as they got used to being apart and became busy with their own lives, but their relationship remained close.

Andrew stopped at the front door and took a serious look around. "There's something Natalie isn't telling me," he vocalized, after she had gone inside.

Narrowed eyes scanned the perimeter, searching for anything out of place before retiring inside.

After Andrew disappeared behind the closed front door, the mysterious figure carefully slid back up from a crouched position in the car's front seat. "How dare he touch her!"

The crazed stalker seethed through gritted teeth as he threw his binoculars down in a jealous rage. He had followed them from the hospital and staked out in front of an empty house for sale a few houses down from Natalie's mother. The lots were large and wooded, giving him obscurity. He wasn't sure about his next move, but whatever it was, would have to wait until her overprotective brother left.

"At least that fucking dog isn't here," he quipped. "I've got to find a way to be with her that won't rouse suspicion," he mused out loud, impatiently waiting for the right opportunity. Meanwhile, he stealthily made his way into the denseness of the trees surrounding Louise's house and surveilled Natalie with her mom and brother.

Their mother made their favorite dinner; fried chicken with mashed potatoes and biscuits. They all knew it wouldn't win a health award, but was perfect comfort food. She didn't have time to make dessert, but they were too full, anyway. Besides, they had wine.

"I'd rather drink my calories for dessert!" Natalie proclaimed.

They sat on the back deck, gazing at the stars in the evening's coolness, wearing sweaters and tucking blankets around their legs. Sage nestled herself into Natalie's lap, enjoying the opportunity to sit outside. Rustling in the brush caused Natalie to freeze as the sensation of ice coursed through her veins, anticipating someone to jump out and grab her. A robust raccoon ambled out, looking for remnants from the bird feeder.

Natalie clutched her chest and released her breath in relief. "Oh, phew, it's just a killer coon," she poked fun at herself.

Natalie's mom and Andrew each reached out and held one of Natalie's hands. "It's going to take time, sweetheart," Louise reassured. "Be patient with yourself."

"That is not one of my virtues, but I'll try."

As they sat and caught up with each other's lives, Natalie was sure the raccoon had friends in the woods watching. She was grateful for her brother's presence.

Sleep was fitful, despite taking her anxiety medication. "I should have asked Ed what he used to knock me out," Natalie grumbled. "Oh, my God, Nat, that's not even funny," she chastised herself. Sage jumped on the bed and nestled against Natalie, reducing her anxiousness.

Once sleep finally came, it was not peaceful.

"Lisa?" Natalie called out, but could not see her friend. Lisa's presence was there, though, and Natalie could sense it.

"Run!" She heard Lisa's voice urge in her mind.

Natalie looked about frantically, panic filling her senses. One of Lisa's paintings hung on the wall in a bedroom Natalie did not recognize. The room was large and handsomely decorated, with a sitting area off to the side. Behind two leather chairs hung a sword collection. Natalie recognized three of them from her previous visions. She withdrew the fourth sword from the wall, feeling the need for protection. The weapon made her hands tingle as if it were conveying a message. Natalie surveyed it, noticing the weapon wanted her to use it to execute a task.

"Save yourself!" Lisa's voice pleaded.

Natalie went to the locked door. Reaching out, she pulled the handle, but it wouldn't budge. Setting the sword on the floor, she used both hands to wrestle the locked door handle. Pulling with all her strength, she fell to the ground. The door was unlocked from the opposite side. Towering above her stood a black demon with red eyes and a wicked smile, revealing dagger sharp teeth. As she grasped for the sword, a clawed foot stamped down on her hand, searing her skin. An evil laugh rang in her ears, drowning out her screams.

Andrew and his mom burst through the bedroom door to Natalie's former childhood room at the sound of her shrieks. Natalie sat in her bed, holding her left wrist where a red burn was visible. Her eyes were wild with disbelief and horror as she struggled to reconcile how a nightmare could leave a physical injury.

"What the hell, Nat?" Andrew's voice was full of tension.

Natalie's mother's hand flew to cover her mouth as she recognized what had happened. "Oh my God, you have the gift," she whispered, loud enough to be heard.

Natalie raised her eyebrows in sarcasm. *"This is a gift?"* she replied with a hint of anger in her voice, as she raised her burned hand in protest.

Louise met her daughter's eyes with somber emotion as her shoulders sagged with regret. "I'm so sorry, my love. I should have helped you all these years, especially when you were a child and had horrible nightmares. I don't know if you remember, but you suffered injuries from them, too. Your Native American ancestors passed down tales of such nightmares. You clearly inherited the ability for Astral Travel, with expanded capabilities only gifted to a few humans. When you stopped having nightmares as a child, I assumed you were safe. I was so wrong. Please forgive me," she pleaded with a quivering chin and eyes brimmed with tears.

Relief flooded Natalie. "You mean you can explain all of this?! Holy shit, mom, I've been thinking I was losing my mind! I've been questioning my sanity, for God's sake!" A choked laugh escaped her as a slight smile appeared. *"I'm not crazy, I'm just special!"* She joked to the heavens, unsure if she felt relief, anger, curiosity, or insanity. "I need an ice pack and an enormous cup of coffee, please. I can't wait to hear all about this!" she ruefully exclaimed.

Chapter 14

The living room was the most comfortable place to hold a deep conversation. Louise had remodeled the house recently, and it reflected her newfound personality instead of her deceased, overbearing husband's. Cheery yellows and blues with scattered florals appeared more like a picture from Southern Living Magazine.

"I love what you've done with the place, mom!" Natalie admired as she took in the surroundings from the comfort of an overstuffed white chair placed in front of a large picture window. Sage sat on the wide ledge of the windowsill with her tail swishing, watching birds and squirrels out front. Rain was falling, making the grass and trees glisten, heightening the scent of pine and earth. Andrew stoked a fire in the fireplace before getting settled in the matching chair to the other side of Natalie, preferring a line of sight outside.

"I wasn't in a good head space yesterday, so I barely noticed anything–not that I'm waking up with a better mentality today," she muttered, while blowing on a steaming cup of coffee.

"Sweetheart, I realize I have caused our strained relationship," Louise jumped right in to an explanation. "I have been working hard through counseling and have been consulting with your friend, Ben, whom you speak so highly of. It has been fascinating to learn more about our Native American practices and beliefs! It would be fun if we can all do something together with Ben and talk to our Spirit Guides!"

Natalie choked on her coffee. "So, this is going to be a day of surprises and revelations, I see! Ben never mentioned this to me! Well, of course he wouldn't… I'm supposed to work this out with you, not him," She muttered to herself. "And working with Ben does not differ from working with me; it's confidential," she added. "Wow, mom, I'm pleasantly shocked and so proud of you! I have so much I would love to understand, especially our religious upbringing someday."

Natalie's mother had been an only child, raised by stern parents, who offered little affection. Most of her childhood was gratefully spent amongst aunts, uncles, and cousins who enabled Louise to learn of her family heritage and experience acceptance. A dutiful daughter, however, sought the same rigidity from an austere husband. His death culminated with strained relationships with her children and propelled Louise to acknowledge the familial pattern she had repeated and seek change within herself.

Louise smiled, and Natalie noticed how her mother carried herself with more confidence and a sense of peace. "Thank you, honey. I'm proud of myself, too. Accepting ownership of my shortcomings and learning the lessons from them, and from your father has made me a better person and, I pray, a better mother. I want the chance to have a good relationship with you two," she pleaded, looking from Natalie to Andrew. "There is so much to heal for all of us."

"I would love nothing more," Natalie sincerely smiled. Whoever this new mother is, I like her! Natalie inwardly thought with an amused smile on her face. It will be nice if we really can have a relationship, but I'm going to be cautiously optimistic for now. There's a lot she and I need to mend with each other.

"Thanks, mom," Andrew answered with a smile, slightly uncomfortable with the emotional seriousness.

"Well, let's start with our heritage. I was never permitted to share or acknowledge what has led to your nightmares. There is much to convey, but this takes precedence," Louise noted, eyeing the bag of frozen peas on her daughter's hand.

Natalie stared intently at her mother, anxiously awaiting to know the story behind her troubling ability.

"My grandparents, aunts, and uncles passed down tales of our heritage and beliefs. The lore surrounding dreams always fascinated me most." she said, with a wistful look on her face. "Native Americans hold the dream state in high regard," Louise began.

Natalie noticed the energy shift in the room, as though surrounded by ancient wisdom. She looked around, wondering if she could glimpse orbs or images. Flashes of blue appeared in the fire, making her wonder if it was a conduit for their energy. Natalie was confident her mother was getting her wish, without realizing it as their Spirit Guides converged around them, creating the shift in vibration. They always seemed to show up and leave signs.

"They believe dreams enable us to travel to other realms where we can communicate with ancestors, spirit guides and animals."

Natalie's mind instantly flashed to Monet, remembering a dog or wolf in each nightmare. Ben's words once again echoed in her mind, *"She will never leave you."*

"Our bodies remain on Earth as we sleep. It is our souls that disconnect and travel, undergoing these experiences."

"So, our dreams are real?" Andrew asked.

"Native Americans do not write their stories or beliefs on paper, but pass them down through tales and by word of mouth. Legend has it that in family history, our souls carry back the information and process it through our human minds in the form of dreams. They encouraged native Americans to remember their dreams so they can learn the lessons the soul brings back for them. Actually, they believe that all on Earth is a dream we are living; nothing is permanent."

"This doesn't sound like my nightmares, so far, except they seem real and I bring back injuries," Natalie chimed in as she lifted the bag of peas to examine her hand.

"Based upon stories I heard growing up, there are those who can travel in time to events that have occurred. The energy still exists in your cells and your DNA from these lifetimes. Actually, it exists for all of us, but a select few bring back physical reminders of their travel. It is considered a rare gift to possess this ability. Of course, with our religious beliefs, we never considered it a gift, sadly."

"I beg to differ that is a gift," Natalie quipped.

Andrew emitted an amused yet sarcastic snort.

"How long has it been since the nightmares began?" Her mom asked, concerned.

"Maybe about two months. They started off vague but have been getting really detailed. It's almost as if I recognize the people in my dreams. Not necessarily the way they look, although sometimes there's something familiar, but more how they act; the roles they play."

The expression of astonishment on her mother's face made Natalie suspect Louise knew something pertinent about what her daughter was experiencing.

"Last night's was completely different, though. There weren't any people in it, only Lisa's voice. She was warning me. I was in a bedroom with a locked door, which could be a projection from my recent, uh, 'experience'."

Andrew's jaw clenched at the reminder of his sister's recent ordeal.

"Oh, and I had a sword that I took from the wall. There were three other swords I recognized from my past nightmares." Natalie entered a trance-like state as she recalled the details of her dreams.

"This sword wanted me to use it, but I couldn't get the door open. I was pulling on it when I fell back as it opened from the other side." she described, mimicking the action of turning a door handle and then falling backwards.

"A black demon with red glowing eyes and razor-sharp teeth stood in the door menacing me. I reached for the sword, when it stepped on my hand with its clawed foot. That's how I got the burn. I don't understand why the burn appears in real time."

Natalie's eyes had become round and filled with terror at the recollection as she remained staring off into space. She mindlessly rubbed the back of her hand, which brought her back to the present.

"The burn is fading. This same thing happened with my other nightmares. The injuries faded throughout the day."

"Natalie," Mom cautioned, "There's more to the gift than injuries. You may find yourself projecting into other people's nightmares, eventually. The gift is bestowed upon a person with the intent that they help others to learn the lessons of their past. It is bequeathed upon a highly evolved soul. First, you will conquer your own lesson."

"Oh no! No, no, no!" Natalie wagged her index finger back and forth and shook her head. *Too much to handle*, echoed in her mind.

Andrew grew pale at the thought of being unable to guard his sister if she began jumping into people's dreams.

"Your soul agreed to this, my child. You are a Dream Warrior. It is a high honor. You would have learned and progressed much sooner had I not permitted your father to intimidate me into silence." Louise admitted with a hint of bitterness, "That was my lesson, though, and I truly believe all happens as it should in its own time."

"I believe that, too. And I believe everything you've told me because it resonates and I can understand its truth in my core. I need to learn all of this, though."

"It is time for you to work closely with Ben." Her mother counseled.

Natalie texted Ben as they sat together, contemplating the information. "We begin tomorrow," Natalie announced, reading his response. "This will be good. It can help me process what just happened and gain control over these nightmares that have turned my life upside down. I got an email from my boss last night urging me to take medical leave, so I think I'll take her up on it."

"I'll reach out to my C.O. about that job we talked about if you're still interested," Andrew interjected.

"It wouldn't hurt to check it out. If it's meant to be, it will happen. How about some breakfast and then I go get Monet? I've got a lot to sort out today."

Her brother's stomach audibly growled in

agreement, the same as when they were kids.

"Well, some things never change," their mother joked as she and Natalie headed into the kitchen.

Glancing out to see how much rain had fallen, Andrew made a mental note of an SUV passing by. They could be going slow because of the weather, he thought to himself, or someone could be staking us out. Either I'm paranoid or hanging around Natalie has my intuition charged up again.

The black Range Rover crept past Louise's house. Its driver noting the occupants just inside the large front window. He wore sunglasses and a cap, in case anyone caught a glance, and noticed Andrew staring straight at him as he drove by. There was no plan. He only wanted to catch sight of Natalie and see what she was doing. The rain most likely meant she wouldn't be venturing out, but he would stay close, anyway. As luck would have it, Natalie emerged in her mother's Subaru an hour later. He kept a safe distance, wondering where they were going.

Chapter 15

"Ouch, this whiplash really hurts," Natalie complained as she was driving.

She was thankful to be away from everybody and have some time to herself to process her concerns. Natalie needed more clothes from her residence and had neglected to get Monet's food when they stopped by on the way home from the hospital. Andrew argued about letting her make the trip alone, but their mother resolved it by taking Natalie's view.

Once again, it felt like a dream as she parked the car and wandered to her apartment. Although it had merely been three days since she had left her home, so much had developed. It seemed like a lifetime. Paranoia became second nature as she looked around for a stalker. *Ed is in police custody*, she reminded herself. *That real life nightmare is over!* The information Louise had shared about the dreams made Natalie certain the other stalker was in her dreams. Something Ben had said confirmed that idea; "He is a wolf in sheep's clothing that walks with you through time." *Hopefully, I'll find out for certain tomorrow, when I see Ben.*

The notebook was sitting on the dining room table with the note from Lisa tucked inside. Natalie crumpled it and hurled it in the trash, as well as the fateful list she had prepared about Jared and her nightmares. Unfortunately, she didn't go over it first to refresh her memory. After Lisa's attitude and failure to acknowledge her texts or calls, Natalie's brain was a jumbled mess.

The ringing of her doorbell startled Natalie from her thoughts. Dread filled her thoughts of explaining the crash and kidnapping to a well-meaning friend, stopping by to check on her. I can see the front door camera on my phone! she remembered. Doing her best to make out the face through the cracked screen, Natalie's heart stopped at the sight of Jared. "What the hell is he doing here?!" she wondered out loud. "Maybe he has a message from Lisa!" Hope overrode the rest of the uncomfortable feelings he elicited, so she opened the door.

"I have to admit, I never would have expected you to come to my apartment," Natalie greeted Jared with an honest statement. "Not alone, anyway. Where's Lisa?"

"Hey! You look stunning," he replied. His eyes assessed every inch of Natalie's face and body, making her insides melt. "I'm sorry to just drop in, but I don't have your number. Lisa has been away at some art exhibit. She mentioned before she departed there would be bad cell reception. I haven't had contact with her, not that we connect every day. I wanted to check in and see how you are managing. I noticed on the news what happened and came by to support you. Do you require anything? May I come in?"

Natalie's intuition threw up a red flag, but curiosity about Lisa won the decision-making process.

Standing aside, she opened the door further to let him inside.

"Where's Monet?" Jared asked, putting his palms up for expression. "I was expecting her to rip my face off."

"At the vet. She was hurt in the car crash. I'm going to pick her up after I leave here."

"What do you mean after you leave? Are you staying someplace else?"

"Yeah, I'm leaving to spend some time with my mother. It's better to have company around for a while."

"Of course, I can imagine. I'm sorry to hear about

what transpired. Are you okay?"

"At the moment I am, but reality hasn't settled in yet. I predict I'll have good and bad days. Thanks for asking."

"Yeah, sure," He answered, moving in closer.

Natalie sidestepped him and walked to the kitchen for a glass of water.

"Did Lisa say anything about me?" She called over her shoulder. "Do you know if she's still mad at me?"

"Mad at *you?*" He repeated, sounding incredulous. "She's worried sick about you. Why would she be mad?"

"After your date together, she found some things I wrote and left mad. We texted the next morning, but even that wasn't pleasant and I haven't heard from her since. Not even after I got into a car crash and was kidnapped! It's quite suspicious." Anger resurfaced within Natalie again at Lisa's behavior.

"I believe you have the wrong impression about me and Lisa," Jared approached her in the kitchen, blocking Natalie in. "I haven't seen her since our date and I've only talked to her once since then, and that was to ask about another painting. We're not a couple! There is no commitment; we keep each other company from time to time. That's *it!*"

Natalie arched her eyebrows and cocked her head sideways at him. "Lisa referred to you as her boyfriend. You two need to get on the same page."

Irritation flashed across Jared's face as he adamantly stated, "I don't appreciate Lisa making something out of nothing, especially when it interferes with what I really want."

"And what might that be?"

"You," His husky voice rasped.

Natalie's heart stopped as her stomach fell to her feet.

"Can we talk? I have some things I would like to share with you." Jared's throaty timbre was driving Natalie's senses wild.

"Sure, I guess. Would you like something to drink?" Natalie struggled to ask without sounding like a porn star.

"Got a beer? I'm sure hot and could use something refreshing."

"I bet you are," she responded, playing on his words. Natalie walked mindfully to her refrigerator to grab the last beer, stunned by what was happening. She poured herself a glass of wine first before strutting her hips back over to the kitchen counter bar top.

"Here ya go! Hope it's cold enough for you. I wouldn't want you to be so hot you are dripping sweat over your nice blue shirt."

Jared winked as he held the base of the beer bottle with a firm grip. An unusually warm and humid day caused sweat to drip down the bottle. Natalie tried to ignore the fact the beer bottle was phallic looking and Jared's fingers were rubbing it up and down.

Sheesh girl stop looking, she thought. It's just wet, that's all. His fingers are slipping. I need this glass of wine more than I imagined. Natalie's sultry full lips kissed the edge of the glass, tipping it methodically as the elixir wet her tongue. She noticed Jared was watching her every move. It enticed her even more.

"Wow Nat, you really make that wine look sensuous while swallowing it. Maybe I should have had wine with you,"

Natalie giggled subtly and wondered why the heck was she being so coy.

"So, what did you want to talk about, Jared?"

"I noticed you have a really cool, slender and sleek sword hanging up. Do you collect sharp objects or was it a gift?" he ignored her question. Something Natalie noticed he was good at, evading things and being mysterious. I suppose he is the type of guy who likes to play with women, entered her mind.

Natalie walked over to the wall and removed the sword from a hook that held it by the hilt. "It's something my grandfather found half buried in a former Civil War field. The blade broke, so he had it cut down and shaped," she explained, stroking the blunt blade. "It's not sharp enough to do much harm, but it's a great conversation piece."

As she turned around to hang it back up, Jared had snuck up behind her, startling her. The sword dropped from her hand and crashed on the floor.

"Sorry, I didn't mean to startle you."

Natalie bent over as Jared watched her curvaceous body and round backside grab his attention.

Damn, it's about time I got her, alone! I really would love to......

Just then, Natalie began talking about Lisa.

"Natalie, I didn't come here to talk about Lisa," as he stepped closer, wrapped his muscular hands around her waist, and looked deep into her startlingly blue eyes, which made her nervous.

"Excuse me, I need another sip of my wine," pushing him away, rushing over to the counter where she left her glass. Jared chuckled and followed her as if he was a cat/dog in heat.

In her thoughts, she was fantasizing, wondering what it would be like to be in his arms. It has been so long since she was in a relationship, the touch could be fantastic. She glanced over to Jared and noticed he was stripping her clothes off with his eyes. While it made her uncomfortable, something was comfortable, familiar, and intriguing about it all. *Who cares about Lisa, the bitch doesn't want to talk to me, anyway. It's free game.*

Just then, she got distracted when the phone rang…. As her heart was pounding from the feelings surging inside her, she answered the call.

It was Andrew. "Everything is good. Thanks for checking on me. I will connect with you real soon, I promise, just busy at the moment. Ok, bye."

"Where were we?"

Jared stood up and said, "Let me remind you." The heat from his hands felt powerful and intimidating around her waist. Her knees trembled and her lips quivered, questioning what was happening. Passion or Pain, a flash through her head. She wanted to just say "take me," but that's not ladylike or appropriate.

Their breathing got heavier as he leaned into her, touching her cheeks and running one hand through her hair, pulling it sensuously. This is hot! I think I like a little of his rough masculine teasing.

Jared sensed she was into it and pulled her in closer, so she could feel how hot he really was. His body was pulsating, sweaty and pumping so fast he just wanted to throw her on the couch. Instead, he would be a gentleman, knowing Natalie would probably scream if he was too rough… at first. Their breathing was deeper and syncing together as one, and the heat was building. Wow, he is well endowed, she thought, as he rubbed up against her.

Natalie doubted herself, but intrigued by all of this. It intoxicated her in a new sense, impulses running through her body like electricity and wondering what it would be like to have sex with him. The electricity was potent. I have to stop thinking so much and allow myself to surrender.

He could feel her curiosity. There was a knowing on some level, and she could not resist his charm. He pulled her wavy hair back a little and pulled it again, cocking her head just enough to kiss the front of her neck and chest. She was feeling helpless, and he sensed it. OMG, I can't control myself, as she grabbed on to him tightly, moaning from his wet kisses and warm hands and grinding her body up against his. Everything in her body tingled.

No one had ever elicited such passion within her and made her feel helpless to control herself. The intoxication blinded her to rational thought. She gave in to the impulses she felt since first laying eyes on him. They had a deeper connection than words could explain. Scooping her up, he seductively slipped her top off her shoulder, exposing her tanned, beautiful, silky skin. "I want to eat you," as he spanked her butt gently. Natalie surprised, and aroused, she could not identify where it came from. At this moment didn't really care either. His dominating energy was hot, and it turned her on.

"Ahh, you are mine Natalie! I have wanted you for many lifetimes. Can't you feel it too?"

"Yes, yes!" she moaned as he threw her on the bed, ripped off her clothes and kissed her luscious body from head to toe. Natalie was in ecstasy, drifting away, far away, but where? Was she drugged again?

Every cell, every nerve, was tingling and even though he was rough, he was masterful at pleasing her, making her crazy, wanting more. "More Jared, don't stop, give me more!"

"Ahh, you like it a little hard and rough, my goddess, queen and slave, don't you?"

There was no stopping now. Natalie was 'hooked' and even though she had a foreboding sensation, the climax was so intoxicating she would let him do anything. And he did. Did he drug me, a brief thought entered her mind, when in an instant they simultaneously climaxed with synchronous screams of ecstasy and all thoughts faded away into oblivion.

Was Pandora's box literally opened, as she lay in the afterglow of this titillating erotica that one only reads about in a book. Jared still pressed up against her body, drooling like a dog and satisfied like King Henry. She wasn't as satisfied as she had imagined. The thought of entering a relationship with Jared gave her a vibe that almost scared her out of her own skin. How can this be? I just had the best orgasm in my entire life!

Into dream land Jared floated while Natalie jumped up to shower. She locked the bathroom door and allowed the hot, steamy water to cleanse her. What was I thinking? I wasn't, that's the problem, she silently scolded herself. What am I going to say or do now? Sleeping around is not who I am, even though I admit it was the best sex I've ever had. A sultry smile, a giggle and onto business as the soap ran down her silky bronzed body. Taking the shower head, she looked down at her legs and saw deep scratches on them. Wow, how did this happen? I never felt him scratch me so deep. Was I that far out of my body? A droplet flowed from her eye, knowing it would disappoint her daddy. So what? I wanted to sleep with him since the first time I laid eyes on him.

How many issues she solved in the shower always astounded Natalie. Feeling more confident after cleaning up, she opened the door with a robe wrapped around herself and searched for fresh clothes.

"My queen, I've been craving more of you," as he tapped his hand on the mattress. "Come back to me," he seductively invited her.

"I've got to pack and get to the vet before they close," Natalie firmly replied, almost cold and aloof.

"What's the matter, didn't you enjoy being my sex slave?"

Picking up Monet's food, ignoring his comments, she was eager to get out of the house.

"You don't waste time, do you?" He cautiously commented, sensing a change in Natalie's demeanor.

"Like I said, I've got to get Monet before the vet closes. They leave early on weekends."

"When can I see you again?" Jared reached out to stroke her face.

Natalie intercepted his hand and guided it back to his side. "You need to leave now and I am truly sorry."

Jared interrupted, "I've wanted you since I laid eyes

on you." His eyes hinted at a crazed obsession.

Natalie looked at the amulet Ben had given her and it was glowing. An uneasy feeling washed over her. "Listen, Jared, I can sense you are also intuitive, and you felt my attraction. That was amazing sex, but I'm good now and we both must go. Honestly, I remember little of it and I can't explain, but whatever the intense draw was to you, I am satisfied." Gosh, I sound like a cold bitch or whore, she thought.

Tension was building between the two of them, while a sense of urgency was rising. The amulet was hot against her chest now. Jared's face instantly flared with anger and his energy felt dangerous. Natalie sensed a crisis. The doorbell rang. Jared went to pull Natalie back, but she escaped his hold and swiftly opened the door to find her neighbor standing there.

"Oh my God! You're safe!" the young woman wailed, throwing her arms around Natalie.

Natalie hugged her in return, relieved at the timely interruption, even though she never met this woman before.

"Yes, I'm okay! Thank you so much for looking in on me! I was just leaving before the vet closes."

"Do we need to be worried here in our apartment complex? I heard someone captured you," the neighbor anxiously inquired.

"No, it was a patient of mine and he's in custody. You're safe," Natalie reassured as she wheeled her suitcase outside with Jared following. "Why don't you walk with me to my car, and I'll fill you in?" she cleverly suggested, turning to lock the door.

"Oh, I would love to know!" the nosy neighbor declared.

Jared's face was like a burning volcano waiting to erupt. Natalie turned to him. "Thank you for checking on me. I've got it from here." She smiled tersely at Jared, making her way to the parking garage with her neighbor in tow, chatting incessantly.

His expression reminded her of someone, but she couldn't place it. Her mind flashed to a nightmare, with Abdul glaring at her, urging her to get away quickly. Natalie shook it off and looked gratefully at the unsuspecting neighbor, who had impeccable timing.

Seething with anger and a desperate desire to have Natalie back, Jared pounded the steering wheel in his car, bursting blood vessels in his hands. Damn! They stung and swelled instantly as he roared out loud in fury. "You are mine and this is not how it ends!" He bellowed into the ethers. "I'm not done with you yet! You will always be mine! We consummated our love today and I know you felt it," he screamed.

While waiting at the counter in the vet's office, a chill went up her spine, foreshadowing a warning. The amulet glowed once again, conveying its own prediction. She mindlessly pressed her hand over it and feared, "Oh, God, what have I done?!"

Chapter 16

I knew I was alive, but what about Monet?
Natalie remembered as she clenched the steering wheel
on her way to the reservation where Ben lived. *It has
only been three days since I made this drive and yet so
much has happened; it feels like a lifetime ago.* The roads
were quiet as Sunday worshippers spent their morning
in church. She knew the site of the crash was coming
up when she noticed her breathing got heavier. The
trauma was fresh and she never really had time to process
anything; it still weighed heavily upon her. *There it is,*
she thought, surprising herself as she pulled off the road
to investigate the area. Trembling as memories flashed in
her head, Natalie swung her legs out of the car and onto
the wet grass. Her knees were shaking and her legs felt
weak, even though it was quiet and peaceful. Proceeding
slowly, images clashed in her mind; a deer on the road,

Monet looking over at her and screams that filled her ears when the airbags deployed, pinning her against the seat. The sound of metal crunching made her body flex and cringe as her car rolled over and collided with the trees. Her amulet was now glowing again and getting hot. I remember this happened that day, it nearly burnt my chest, she reminisced. But where is Monet? She panicked, placing her hand over her mouth and looking around, confused. *Monet is trapped! I have to get help and get her out!* hearing the whimpering sounds and moans of her injured partner. As Natalie spun around, she regained present consciousness and remembered Monet was injured and at the vet for a few days. Now her mom was taking care of her. *I guess it's a gift not to remember too much right now;* she admitted as she walked somberly back to the car, turning her head over her shoulder one more time, thankful she was headed to Ben for help now. *Gosh, I hope he can help me solve some of these puzzles.*

Rain drizzled down upon the black tar roads making the drive feel mysterious as the clouds covered the sky. *Oh, dear God, please let me arrive safely. I cannot take another trauma,* she prayed. Her knuckles were turning white from squeezing the steering wheel so intensely, thinking. *This drive is going to feel long.*

Natalie was intent on driving cautiously as she

went deeper into the countryside. The trees were bigger and sparkled with the raindrops in a magical way. Her headlights were on just in case anything jumped out of the woods, so perhaps she could avoid an incident. Her anxiety was building as she became impatient to get to Ben's house. *There it is thank goodness,* she thought. The driveway was gravel. As she drove up to the house, she could see Ben rocking in his chair under the covered front porch, waiting for her arrival. A deep sigh released tension as her shoulders dropped. She felt safe now and ready to spend some time with this wonderful wise man.

Ben observed the strain apparent on Natalie's face and in her body language. Her energy felt heavy to him as he meditated the night before to prepare for their sessions today. It was a welcome sight to see her.

"You are weary, my child." He embraced her quickly and rushed her out of the rain.

"Much weighs on my mind," Natalie responded as she took his hand and walked up the steps.

Ben outstretched his arms once they were inside, and Natalie found comfort in the embrace of a trusted friend and guide. Anxiety drained from her, knowing answers would be found and she was not alone.

"I am grateful to the Spirits you are alive."

"As am I! They've had their hands full looking after me lately!"

He patted her arm, an endearing sign he cared. Natalie was always curious where he picked up this habit, it felt good each time, like an old friend.

After Natalie filled him in on events, revelations, and details, they decided it was time to get to work.

"We will begin with a past life regression. Your nightmares and kidnapping have a common thread of behavior. It has been permitted to happen worldwide in cultures and in family dynamics. We must ask if you are the chosen one to break the pattern in this lifetime and determine the common theme."

"I think the theme is pretty obvious," Natalie sarcastically retorted, with a playful smile on her face.

"Based upon the details of your nightmares and Mr. Bowden's behavior, I expect you're right! Let's find out, though, if a memory of a past life is similar to your nightmares."

Natalie believed she understood where Ben's line of thinking was going, but wanted to see what came of the regression before solidifying her thought. This was the first time she was going to experience a regression and, with a little apprehension, was also excited to solve the mystery.

"Ok, ready," she proclaimed, closing her eyes while lying on the couch, wearing an eye mask.

"You will be aware of some of what happens, Natalie, and you may remember most of the details, but I will record it as well."

Ben led Natalie through the hypnosis process. He guided her through a process of deep breathing and counting backwards slowly.

A soft, reassuring voice prompted questions as Natalie was in an altered consciousness to access her memories.

"Look down at your feet. What do you see?"

"My feet are bare."

"What is under your feet?"

"Dirt. It's everywhere."

"How are you feeling?"

"I feel anxious."

What color is your skin?"

"Brown."

"Do you get a sense if you are a male or female?"

"I am female."

"Look at what you are wearing. What does it look

like?"

"It's a wrap."

"Can you describe it and what else you're wearing?"

"It has a tribal print on it. I am also wearing necklaces and bracelets made of shells and beads."

"What do your surroundings look like?"

"There are thatch huts in what looks like a small village surrounded by trees. It is dry and dusty. My fellow villagers are brown, too. The other women are dressed similarly to me."

"Can you describe anything about your life there?"

"The women have an outdoor common area where we cook together. I live with some of the women."

"Are you married?"

"Yes. The women I live with are my husband's other wives."

"How are you feeling here in the village?" Natalie paused for a moment as she connected with her feelings.

"There is tension."

"What is there tension from?"

"Soldiers who raid the village. We know they will

rape, mutilate, or kill us. We look out for each other, except for one wife. She is jealous of me."

"Have you ever seen her before this lifetime?"

"I recognize her energy. She travels with me through time. She is envious of the attention my husband shows me. I do not like his excessive attention, but there is no escape for me."

"Do you recognize your husband?"

"I have seen my husband before. I recognize his jealous behavior. He hits me for behavior he imagines in his mind." Natalie's breathing became erratic, so Ben redirected her.

"Natalie, take a nice deep breath and relax, you're safe with me. Does your husband have any distinguishing marks?"

"Yes, he has a scar on his cheek."

"What is your relationship like with your husband?"

"At first, we were irresistibly attracted to each other, but then he became abusive and possessive. Now I fear him." Tears escaped from the corners of Natalie's eyes.

"You're doing great, Natalie. Are you okay to continue?"

Natalie nodded her head in affirmation.

"Do you recognize anyone else?"

"The Medicine Man. He is kind to me, like a father or a good friend. I have felt his caring before."

"Let's fast forward to your death in this lifetime. How did you die?"

Natalie began to hyperventilate. "Soldiers have invaded the village! One of them has a machete to my breast! My husband sliced his throat from behind, but accuses me of enjoying the soldier's touch. He uses the machete to slice my throat!" Screaming, Natalie woke as Ben guided her from the hypnotic state.

Natalie took in her surroundings after removing the eye mask, reminding herself she was safe. Ben guided her through a calming breathing exercise to bring Natalie back into her body.

"Was the past life regression similar to your nightmares?"

"Yes, it was almost identical! The energies of the same people I have perceived in my nightmares were there!"

"I think it is safe to say you have not been having nightmares. You have been experiencing past life memories. Your soul is showing you patterns of abuse and oppression which must be broken, not just for you, but for the women of the world."

Natalie's jaw hung slightly open, and her eyes grew wide as the reality of Ben's wisdom dawned on her. Goose bumps covered her flesh as her human mind and soul danced in resonance. That was her body's way of conveying validation or synchronicity.

"What about Ed Bowden and my kidnapping?"

"He is the man with two faces I saw in my vision. He has not traveled with you through time, but is a part of the same lesson in this lifetime. The purpose is to highlight abusive practices against women that have been allowed and accepted. He is linked to you and your past lives through a similarity in behavior and belief. It is time for you to stand in your power against the abuse and help free women of the world from man's domination."

"How were you able to ascertain all of that from a past life reading?"

Ben smiled. "Your reading merely validated what I have been shown. I have spent decades learning to read and understand the energies of the Great Spirit. As a human vessel, we all have individual ways of interpreting Divine messages. First, we must recognize the information we are given and how our human mind construes it. Then we practice with the elders, who teach us how to convey the information into accurate messages. It is imperative one's personal struggles not interfere in our translation from the Great Spirit.

"Ah, that's why my mother said first I must conquer my own lesson." Natalie's eyes lit up with comprehension.

"Yes!" Ben nodded his head vigorously. "You do not want to bring tainted emotion or unprocessed trauma into work done on the behalf of another person." Ben shook his head, indicating grave seriousness.

Natalie gave him a thumbs up. "Getting back to my current situation, there's one slight problem; I don't have a domineering husband in this lifetime. So, how is my current lifetime parallel to past lives?"

"You are taking the roles of previous characters too literally. We all travel together, repeating the same lessons until they are mastered, utilizing a variety of representations. For instance, a woman may take on the role of a chambermaid, a fellow wife, a mother, or… a friend. A male can appear as a manservant, an uncle, a priest, or…"

"A Spiritual Healer!" Natalie finished his sentence with her jaw agape again and blue eyes huge with astonishment. "You were there in all the past lives I believed were nightmares! I'm so new to all of this! Am I living in parallel worlds, astral traveling… what is this?"

Smiling, Ben reached out his hand and patted her on the knee. "I did say we have traveled together through time before," He winked. "It is said time is a manmade construct and we are simultaneously living multiple lives in a parallel existence. Astral travel is when our spirit, also called our astral body, leaves its physical body and moves into another dimension. We do this while lucid dreaming or when in a deeply meditative state. It is therefore possible to astral travel to another dimension or lifetime as you dream. So, the answer to your question is yes."

Natalie jumped up from the couch and began pacing around the living room, threading fingers through her hair as if her head would come off if she didn't keep it attached. "For something completely unbelievable, this makes sense!" Natalie stopped pacing and stared at Ben with a smile of relief on her face. Her energy could be felt shifting into a higher state of vibration as she aligned with the purpose of her life.

As she reflected, things were coming together. Natalie sat down, placed her hands on her cheeks, slightly bent over… thinking, "That's why I'm a psychologist in this lifetime; so I can help women heal and become stronger."

Ben shrugged, "It stands to reason."

"Mom said I may have the capacity to enter other people's nightmares once I learn the lessons of my own. Is that going to happen?"

"Yes, that is your soul contract. You will use your gifts as a trained healer and your gifts as a Dream Warrior to help others learn in the same method you are learning; by taking the experiences of your past lives and healing them in this lifetime to end the cycle."

"Wait, soul contract? What do you mean?"

"Simply put, a soul contract is an agreement between souls to fulfill roles for each other with the purpose of enabling that soul to master a lesson they wish to learn. For instance, a spouse who is unfaithful is helping teach their partner to learn self-love or to set personal boundaries."

Natalie slowly nodded her head in agreement and acceptance.

"Okay, how do I complete my lesson and heal?"

"Let us finish identifying the players in your past life memories. Think back on their characteristics; who is a female that is jealous?"

Natalie contemplated the roles of characters Ben had listed and remembered the last one; friend. Furrowing her forehead, she looked at him in disbelief. "Is it Lisa? Oh my God!"

Ben silently nodded, his face blank.

Standing up from the couch, more curious than ever,

she had so many questions.

Natalie shook her head as if trying to clear it and let out an exasperated sigh. As she considered Lisa's recent jealousy pertaining to Jared and to past boyfriends, the connection clicked. "In my past life memories, she was always jealous of me. The same behavior is repeating itself in this lifetime!"

Natalie pondered her unexplained attraction to Jared. Her expression was awe-stricken as the last and biggest piece of the puzzle fell into place.

Natalie cried out in bewilderment. "Jared was my husband and abuser in every single memory! This explains the psychotic mentality I detect from him! He's infatuated with me to the point of delusion; just like in the nightmares! I had to be attracted to him so we could play out our roles with each other!" The amulet glowed. "This thing is possessed," she declared, looking down at it and holding it between her thumb and index finger.

"Has it glowed before?"

"It glows and is hot when I'm with Jared." She looked at Ben with an astounded expression. "But then it did the same thing when a car drove by while I was examining the scene of my accident. It makes no sense."

"What does Jared drive?"

Natalie's face became alarmed. "Is he following me?! Holy shit! Geez, I am SO naive!"

"Be gentle on yourself. We meet occurrences in our life based upon our own level of integrity and experience. You would never consider menacing another person, nor have you been the object of someone's delirium in this lifetime, so your mind does not lead you to such conclusions. You are a person of honor."

This time, it was Natalie who patted Ben on the shoulder. "Thanks, Ben!" She smiled affectionately. "So what now? How do I end this without losing my life this time?"

"We must help your Soul to heal by retrieving and reuniting it with the fragments that have been lost."

"Is this like a Soul retrieval?"

"Yes. When we suffer an excruciating event, our Soul fragments to protect the human psyche. It remains fragmented in that time and memory until retrieved and reintegrated. In order to bolster your strength and enable healing, we must make you whole again."

Natalie smiled sadly. "My poor Soul must be scattered all over the place. Let's put it back together."

Laying back down on the couch, Ben led Natalie into a trance-like state, narrating to her as he began the journey of regaining the shards of her Soul. Two hours later, the undertaking was complete.

"How do you feel?"

"I feel like a badass because I've got all my pieces back together!" She laughed. "I feel strong and powerful; like my life force has been returned and missing parts of me returned home! Not that I wasn't 'me' before, but I was more passive. I'm not afraid," she comprehended with amazement. "I imagine Wonder Woman feels like this." Natalie stated with a gleam in her eye.

Ben smiled and nodded his head with admiration.

"You are ready to move forward and finish the lesson you came here to master."

Chapter 17

He could spy Natalie, her mother, and brother through the kitchen windows which overlooked the back deck. Binoculars remained trained on Natalie, ogling her bewitching eyes and lips as she helped make dinner. A flood light came on as the back door opened and Monet gingerly hopped down the two steps to the low deck. Upon seeing the protective canine, he crouched behind trees and brush, perturbed the dog could ruin his ability to surveil his object of desire.

"Hop down one more step, big girl," He could hear Natalie say. "You're doing so well on your cast!"

Monet sniffed the air. Hackles raised on her back as she let out a protective growl, catching his scent. Monet lunged towards the trees exactly when Natalie gripped the leash handle tightly, preventing her guardian from running after an unseen entity on her fractured leg. Trepidation absorbed Natalie, who contemplated whether Monet detected a person or a wild animal. Instead of succumbing to fear, she called out for her brother.

"Andrew! Bring your gun!"
Thrashing sounds in the brush caused Monet to bark frenziedly and pull against her leash.

"Andrew!" Natalie thundered.

The back door flew open the second Andrew appeared with his pants barely pulled up. "Are you okay?" he called.

Despite the seriousness of the situation, Natalie burst into laughter at the sight of her bewildered, half-naked brother.

"Natalie! Answer me!" he demanded, pulling his pants up while running towards a frenzied Monet.

"Yes! I'm sorry," she managed through stifled laughter. "There is unmistakably something in the woods, the question is what… or who." She became serious upon finishing the sentence.

Andrew dove into the brush and trees in the direction of Monet's attention. "Whatever it was, it's gone!" he called out. "It's too dark to see anything. I'll come out in the morning and check for foot or paw prints."

"Next time I take Monet out, I'll make sure you're not in the bathroom," she ribbed with a mischievous smile.

"Next time Monet needs to go out, I will be the one taking her!" he insisted, walking out from the woods, pants in their customary fashion.

Natalie rolled her eyes and shook her head, not wanting to instigate an argument.

"What makes you think there's a possibility it was a person out there?"

"Something Ben and I discovered today. I'll fill you and mom in after dinner."

At that point a car could be heard driving away in the distance. Monet continued to pull against her leash, wanting desperately to track down the scent.

"You've chased a car before! That could just be a neighbor, missy!" Natalie wagged a finger at her protector.

Andrew responded with an incredulous look on his face and rolled his eyes. "Do I even want to hear about this?" He threw his hands up in the air with exasperation. Her brother didn't want to wait to hear details, but a growl from his stomach prevented him from pressing the matter.

They retired to their usual places in the living room after a dinner of hearty chili and cornbread.

A bed of blankets had been made for Monet next

to Natalie's chair, while Sage assumed her new favorite spot on the windowsill. Natalie went into detail about the past life regression, the nightmares, and Soul retrieval session.

"Ben was able to help me find out information about my nightmares, which are actually past life memories, and how it correlates with what is happening now. Jared, Lisa, Ben, and I are replaying roles we have shared in past lives together. We will keep replaying them until we learn the lesson they were intended to teach us.

"What is your lesson?" Andrew wanted to know.

"It is my job to stand against abuse and domination from men. However, I am to take what I've learned and teach other women to do the same, to end the cycle of accepted oppressive behavior everywhere," Natalie explained, motioning with her arms to include the entire planet.

"No pressure," Andrew mocked. "But I can see why you need to travel into their dreams to help stop the trend of injustice."

Her mother cocked her head to the side and smiled tenderly, "Ben has been with you in many lifetimes."

Natalie returned the smile, "Yes, he has always looked after me."

"So does he have a lesson too?" Her brother wanted

to know.

Natalie's expression turned thoughtful as she contemplated Ben's role. "My intuition tells me Ben is a Guide or a Guardian who incarnates with me. He's like an Earthbound Angel. I don't know what Jared and Lisa's lessons are; that's for them to decipher. I'm overwhelmed trying to survive my own." Her brow furrowed at her last observation.

Louise was fascinated, yet terrified for her daughter. "In the past life memories, your husband abused and killed you," She reiterated with dismay.

"Yes, mom, he did. This lifetime is very different, though. I'm not married to him and I don't live in a country where my rights and voice are completely disregarded. Women's rights still have a long way to go here, but theoretically, I have a legal leg to stand on. I can fight back this time, end the cycle, and help other women do the same! Humanity can't keep ignoring how women are treated. Now that I know this is my Soul Contract, I won't let them!" Natalie's newfound strength and passion fueled her determination.

"You're sure this Jared guy is the one from your memories?" Andrew's face was taut with malice.

"Yes, I'm sure. Ben's amulet glows in warning when I'm near him. We've had crazy chemistry I can't explain; more so on his part. The guy is fanatical and domineering. His energy is identical to the husbands in my memories." Natalie's eyes became distant as she relived the disturbing memories of Jared's past and current behavior. A shudder of anguish ran through her body. "My body, cells, DNA, and Soul remember it all," she gravely stated, with an undertone of resentment. "Maybe my Soul agreed to learn this painful lesson, but this is where it ends."

"Do you have a plan?" Her military minded brother inquired.

"I have no idea what to expect! I know he's following me. On the way to Ben's, I pulled over to examine my crash site and something happened, giving me a warning, but I didn't recognize it `then."

Her mother audibly caught her breath at the thought of another stalker. Louise visualized her child in a rollover accident, and it struck terror in her heart as she literally felt Natalie's horror. One hand covered her mouth and the other waved Natalie on to continue.

"The amulet started glowing when a black SUV drove by. I thought it was going berserk, but it was actually giving a warning Jared was following me."

Andrew's eyes hardened with rage. "I saw a black

SUV drive by here slowly on Saturday. I bet that was him in the trees when you let Monet out! Son of a bitch!" He pounded a fist into the palm of his other hand. "I'm calling the cops!"

"I'm in the identical situation with this stalker as I was with Ed Bowden! Jared hasn't done anything... yet. My hands are tied and so are the police's!"

Standing up and pacing, Andrew massaged his temples, wracking his brain before retreating into the kitchen.

Louise nervously went to the windows, pulling down shades, imagining someone malicious nestled in the trees watching her and her children. A tremor of alarm ran down her spine as a blanket of foreboding settled within the house.

Her brother could be heard on the phone talking to his Commanding Officer. "I need some time. I've got a situation at home. Thank you, Sir."

Intuition told Natalie the 'situation' would be over sooner than later. Feelings of trepidation and resolve clashed within her. She felt ready, regardless of the outcome.

Natalie paced as she brushed her teeth, feeling like she was on the precipice of bringing a close to lifetimes of agony. Images of the roles she and Ben had played together in their past lives made her heart ache. We've been through so much sorrow! I want to end this for both of us NOW! It seems like I'm about to jump off a cliff. I'll either die in the fall or fly; it could go either way.

A crash in the kitchen sent Andrew and Louise running. Andrew drew his pistol and aimed it in front of himself as he methodically scanned around him and carefully entered the kitchen, motioning for his mother and sister to remain behind.

"Mew!" They could all hear as Andrew lowered his weapon and gave a relieved laugh." The cat knocked over the vase of flowers!" he sarcastically reported.

Their mother ran to get a dustpan while Natalie returned to the bathroom, her mouth foaming with toothpaste. Andrew followed behind her.

"Don't think this is weird, but do you want me to sleep with you in your room?"

Foam sputtered from her mouth as Natalie laughed again at her brother.

"I'll take that as a no." He stifled a smile while walking away.

Bedroom doors were left open, lights turned on and old hunting rifles were brought out from a closet.

"I can't believe you kept these after dad died!" Andrew exclaimed as he examined the rifles he and Natalie were permitted to shoot when they were older.

Their mother rationalized, "Well, as a single woman alone in a house, I want protection! At least with a rifle, I don't have to aim too well!" Louise placed one beside her bed and Natalie took the other.

Andrew had his own pistol that never left his side. He double checked the chamber and made sure all was working properly.

They all felt as though they were going into battle, with no plan of attack.

"We are going to practice shooting tomorrow," Andrew promised. "It's easier to pull a trigger when you know how the gun is going to feel as it fires."

Their mother cringed at the thought, while Natalie felt empowered.

Monet slept on blankets next to Natalie's side of the bed. Natalie felt safer in her presence than with a gun propped up against the nightstand. Sleep was fitful, but not uneventful.

Natalie opened her eyes and took in the surroundings with a twinge of alarm building in her chest. An unseen and malevolent energy permeated the atmosphere. Every step threatened to lure her into peril. She held her tensed hands up in front of her body, ready to defend herself. Bare feet on the cold tile made her tremble, although she didn't think her body was reacting solely to the chilled floor. Mist swirled around her feet as Natalie walked through Lisa's gallery. Eerie lights flickered alternately, casting random shadows on paintings and sculptures, bringing them to life. Natalie felt a tug on her hair and shrieked, spinning around to confront the perpetrator, only to find a statue with its hand sticking out as the culprit. Eyes in paintings followed her from room to room and her spine prickled with the knowing of being watched. A darkened room at the end of a corridor beckoned her to enter. She was able to resist the urge to flee and crept closer to its nebulous entrance. Entranced, Natalie stepped across the threshold. Flaming eyes abruptly opened as Lisa's voice cried, "Run!" An unseen hand wrapped itself around her ankle, pulling Natalie to the floor, filling her with paralyzing terror. She scratched at the tile, unable to gain traction as she was violently pulled towards the source of the demonic eyes. Her hands frantically grasped in the dark, desperately searching for anything to slow her descent into hell. Cold metal met her fingertips and she scrambled for a grasp. The hilt of a sword became one with her hand just as the demon whipped her body up to its hideousness. Natalie swung, screaming with resolve, slicing the beast across the face. The clawed hand released its grasp, sending her falling through space as howls of pain and fury reverberated through the surrounding air.

Natalie sucked in her breath, fighting for air as she felt herself land with a wallop. Laying on her back, head nestled in a pillow, her eyes flew open. Deep breaths brought a racing heart back to normal rhythm. Monet looked up from her blankets and thumped her tail as Natalie peered over the bed. "I escaped this time," she whispered. "But fate has been set into motion, because that dream feels like a warning!" she cautioned. Natalie massaged the pup's oversized ears, finding solace in the beautiful shepherd before attempting sleep again. "Watch out, Jared, this is war! I'll be taking over the direction of my nightmares, thank you!" Natalie defiantly pledged to the ethers. Filled with resolve, she smiled triumphantly, nestled herself into the blankets and wondered what would happen next while she was dreaming.

Chapter 18

"I'm home. We need to talk," Natalie gasped in surprise, not expecting a text from Lisa to be the first thing she saw upon awakening. It roused Natalie and sent her mind into overdrive, nervous in anticipation of what direction their conversation might take. Adrenaline surged to her brain and dispelled the morning fog hanging on from deep sleep.

"Well, this is a lovely way to wake up," Natalie sarcastically informed Monet. "I think I'll have coffee and breakfast before I respond."

"Come on, our little brother has to get out of bed and take you outside," she snickered.

The two cohorts snuck into Andrew's room as he lay sleeping, mouth ajar.

"Give him kisses!" Natalie urged.

Monet licked his face with her large wet tongue, provoking Andrew to swat and yell obscenities.

"Hey, that's no way to greet us!" Natalie giggled. "Monet needs to go out and if I remember correctly, that's now your job!"

"Ugh!" her brother protested, pulling a pillow over his head.

"Fine. I'll take you out, Monet!" Natalie playfully called as the shepherd limped down the hallway.

"I'm coming!" Andrew's muffled voice declared.

Their mother was already in the kitchen, pouring a strong cup of coffee into her favorite blue pottery mug. A pink flannel nightgown and slippers brought Natalie's memories back to childhood, spending Saturday mornings on the couch watching cartoons while her parents read the newspaper. Louise had redone the kitchen cabinets in white, giving the room a clean, airy look. A large window over the sink showed a crystal blue sky.

"Good news, mom! We all survived the night!" Natalie joked, with a hint of sarcasm.

Louise cocked her head to the side and gave Natalie a woeful look. "At least you've still got your sense of humor," she remarked with a smirk.

Her brother shuffled into the kitchen still in his jersey

pajama pants, a T-shirt and flip-flops. "Come on, Monet, let's see who's outside."

The shepherd wagged her tail and followed him outside, sniffing the air and scanning the perimeter, despite having a cast on her front leg.

In the light of day, trees appeared welcoming, instead of sinister from the night before. Natalie supervised Monet around the backyard while Andrew investigated, making sure she didn't run after anything.

Looking down, Andrew observed, "There's too much debris and leaves to see prints."

Natalie chose not to share what intuition told her; someone had been watching. A jolt ran through her body when she realized they were probably being watched right now. Anger surged through her veins. How dare he include my family in this! She fumed.

"Let's do something productive, like drink coffee," she called, heading inside, flipping her middle finger to the bushes in the event someone was there.

Hands wrapped around steaming mugs of coffee, they settled again in the living room, where Natalie revealed Lisa's text.

Agitated, her mother inquired, "That's all she said? 'I'm home and we need to talk?' I would think she'd be concerned."

"Yeah, how about, 'Are you okay? How's my dog? I'm sorry I haven't checked on you after almost dying'..." Andrew chimed in, shaking his head in irritation.

"I'm trying to give her the benefit of the doubt, but I am angry she hasn't responded to any of my texts or at least asked about Monet. This really is unusual, so I want to see her and talk to her before I draw any conclusions."

"You're such a shrink," her brother playfully chided.

Natalie rolled her eyes at her brother. "I also need to let her know what I learned about Jared during the past life reading with Ben. The three of us have been traveling through lifetimes together and he's dangerous. I only know the lifetimes I've had with him, and he has been abusive and violent."

Natalie's mind drifted to her past life regression and its revelations. Guilt and incredulity crept into her bones as thoughts went further back to remember their passionate encounter, knowing she'd have to come clean about it.

"That conversation is going to suck and I hope she's willing to accept what I tell her. I need to warn her today. Just because Jared never harmed her in one of our past lives together, doesn't mean he won't."

Natalie's brow furrowed with concern while her stomach flipped with dread. Details about her sex life, especially a tryst with Jared, she kept private. She sure as hell would not confess to her mother and brother, but had to with Lisa.

"This is some crazy shit," Andrew furrowed his brow and shook his head. "If you weren't my sister, I'd think you are as looney as your patients!"

"My patients are not looney!" Natalie defended, but then thought back to being stalked and kidnapped by one of them. "Well, all but one," she ruefully wrinkled her nose.

"You'll feel better after getting that conversation out of the way. I agree she needs to know. You can go over after breakfast," Louise suggested.

Natalie knew her mother was right, but apprehension made her insides roll with unease. Am I nervous for some other reason? She suddenly wondered as she proceeded with their morning routine, becoming distracted.

"When can I come over?" Natalie's text to Lisa read.

"Now is a good time. Come to the gallery. I'm

painting."

"Ok. I'll leave soon. It will be just us, right?"

"Yes."

"No, Andrew, you cannot come with me!" Natalie argued with her brother as she tried to get in the car alone.

"Then what did I take leave for?!"

"Jared will not kidnap me amidst the River Arts District! It's too crowded! What if he's just infatuated and we're overreacting? I'm going to feel ridiculous if you took leave for nothing! Besides, this is a very private conversation between me and Lisa, and it's going to take a lot of professional maneuvering on my part. I can't focus with you hovering around!"

Andrew contemplated being present for their cat fight with disdain and amended his offer. "Let me drop you off and pick you up, then. It would make me feel like I'm doing something to help you!" he argued.

Exasperated, Natalie let out a sigh. "Fine," she relented, handing him the keys.

No parking spots were available, so Andrew let Natalie out in front of Lisa's gallery and waited for her to go in. She waved to him as the door opened.

"God, I feel like I'm in elementary school again," she complained, closing the door behind her.

"Lisa?!" Natalie called out. "Maybe she's in the back."

Her stomach was already nauseous at the thought of having a confrontation with her best friend. However, an uneasy feeling prickled at the base of her neck, telling her something wasn't right. She plodded through the gallery, feeling as though she was experiencing deja vu. Images from her nightmare flashed in her mind and she instantly feared that perhaps they weren't dreams; what if they were premonitions?

"Run!" she heard Lisa scream as a voice in her head, just as Ben's amulet glowed hot on her chest.

Spinning on her heel to leave, she slammed into Jared.

"Oh God, no!" her mind pleaded, defensively attempting to raise her arms as a barrier, to no avail.

His hand clamped down over her mouth with a cloth soaked in chloroform, covering her nose and mouth. Natalie instinctively screamed beneath it, fiercely writhing to be released. His free arm held her in a vice grip, crushed against his muscular body. Natalie slammed her knee into his groin, giving herself a moment of fresh air as the cloth slipped.

"You want to play with that?" Jared pervertedly

teased, jerking her head to the side and biting her earlobe. Repulsion emboldened her to bite his hand, only fueling his excitement.

"This is more like it!" He sneered with lustful exhilaration. "I have fantasized about sexual combat with you! This is gonna hurt so good!"

Barely breaking arms free, she clawed at his hair and tried gouging his eyes with her thumbs. Jared reaffixed the cloth, succumbing Natalie to the toxin. This can't be happening; I'm supposed to win this time! she thought futilely, sinking into darkness.

When she awoke, Natalie lay spread eagle, hands and feet handcuffed to a bed.

"You fucking son of a bitch!" she screamed while thrashing against the restraints. Angry tears of despair ran down her face while Natalie's thoughts fought against the knowledge he had killed her in lifetimes before. Trembling at the thought of suffering through torture and a violent death by Jared's hand, she sobbed hopelessly.

Double doors to the sizable bedroom opened at once, sending shock waves of fear through Natalie's extremities. Dressed in black leather, including a hooded black leather mask, Jared methodically approached Natalie, his dark eyes crazed as he carnally appraised her. Natalie flashed back to the demon in her nightmare.

"Did I hear tears of joy?" His left hand emerged from behind his back, holding a whip. Crack! It sounded as he snapped the whip above her restricted body, causing her to flinch.

Play the game if you want to survive, Natalie heard a voice advise. She remembered what Ben had told her when she first went to see him about a stalker; "Your strength has not been great enough to defeat him until now. The work you have done in this lifetime will enable you to end this, but it will be dangerous. Great Spirits walk with you, offering their guidance and protection. Call upon them in time of need." She took Ben's advice and prepared herself.

Despite Jared's threatening presence, Natalie closed her eyes and breathed deeply, willing calmness into her body and summoning her spirit to reconnect. Great Spirits, I call upon you for guidance and protection. It is my intention to end this repeated pattern of abuse now... and to survive. And so it is, and so it shall be, she prayed silently. Natalie's life force surged within her essence, giving newfound strength and determination.

Her body tingled with energy, as though she were supernatural. Remember, you have superpowers! Lisa's voice sounded in her head. Natalie smiled slightly at the childhood memory of herself and her best friend coping with the uncertainty of frightful extrasensory gifts.

"A smile graces those luscious lips." Jared's sultry voice snapped Natalie out of her trance, mistaking her smile as meant for him. He traced the outline of her mouth with the cold tip of a sword as her vibrant blue eyes snapped open, a newfound sense of power emanating from them. Jared detected the shift in energy and became more aroused by the challenge her power presented. The whip lay cast aside, traded out for a sword while she connected to Spirit.

Natalie realized she had been in this room before… while she was dreaming. Identical to her nightmare, Lisa's painting hung on the wall. Three swords hung on an opposite wall in a sitting area behind two leather chairs. These chairs housed restraining devices, however. The fourth sword was missing from the collection and Natalie recognized its energy as the one that lay menacingly against her throat. The dreams WERE premonitions, she discerned.

There were more sickening details in the room than her nightmare revealed. This isn't a bedroom, she perceived, this is a torture chamber. Natalie fought to keep her emotions of terror from being visible on her face and from taking over her thoughts.

A variety of weapons and costumes, masks

and hoods adorned the walls. Furniture was sparse, but functional for the perceived needs; a bed, which she already occupied, leather chairs and a table, all with devices of enslavement.

"Do you like my lair?"

"It's impressive," she falsely complemented, feigning to be enthralled.

"You are a maniacal, diseased piece of shit," Natalie desperately wanted to convey. It wouldn't make a difference. A psychopath only values their own opinions. My power lies within myself, so that's where I focus my energy. Regaining her focus, she telepathically communicated to the blade that rested at her neck, "You will be in my hands before this is over."

A tripod with a camera recorded everything, she noticed as she lay handcuffed to the bed.

"Perfect," Natalie murmured.

Jared snarled his lip as he slid the sword beneath her sweater, slicing it open from bottom to top, exposing her lacy bra and toned physique.

"Does imprisoning women and holding them captive excite you?" She voiced for the sake of the camera, hoping it had audio.

"More than you can imagine! Watching again is almost as good as making the video," he sadistically replied, pressing the blade against her torso.

"Am I the first one you've held in bondage against their will?"

Jared scoffed as if insulted. "You are not the first and you won't be the last! However, I do hope you'll be the most memorable."

That's the evidence I needed! She smiled to herself, knowing his narcissism and lust would be his downfall in the end.

Natalie groaned, as though she enjoyed being bound and threatened. She arched her breasts to press harder against the sword. "This will be erotic if I can actively participate," she seductively invited, smiling mischievously.

Jared instantly was overcome with a carnal craving for her. He had to have her that instant and was struggling to maintain control.

"I seem to recall you got what you wanted the last time and discarded me like a used dishrag!" Without realizing it, Jared was searching for a reason to go against his better judgment and free her.

Natalie tilted her head coyly against the pillow and

arched her eyebrow provocatively. "Jared, that's part of the game, isn't it? What fun would it be if we had sex and then I fawned all over you? You have to chase me!" She writhed her body tantalizingly, attempting to further stimulate his sexual yearnings and override his discernment.

Jared couldn't resist his urges any longer. He knew Natalie was right handed, so came around the bed to unlock the left handcuff. She was correct; a limited opportunity to interact would make it more stimulating. He tossed the sword onto the vacant side of the bed, where it landed with a thump. It might come in handy later.

With her newly freed hand, she tore the mask from his face and head, making his appearance less frightening. Her fingers rubbed roughly against his lips, tantalizing him as she flirtatiously ran her tongue across her own. Jared straddled her, bending over and crushing her mouth with his. Natalie whimpered beneath him, urgently returning his fervor. The right handcuff clanged against the bed frame as she pulled at it, indicating she needed use of her hand to further titillate his senses.

Jared hesitated, questioning if it would be wise to unlock her any further. Not wanting to give him time to think, she reached down with her free hand and stroked vigorously between his thighs. Moaning with satisfaction, he stretched above her to unlock the second handcuff.

Using her psychological skills to be cunning, Natalie gained one more step towards freedom.

Both hands free, Natalie sat up and removed a ruined sweater. Jared held her close, unfastened her bra, and then forcefully pushed her back down. Attempting to maintain a modicum of control, Natalie extended her arms and began fondling his breasts, giving her mind time to think.

Holy shit, I'm actually getting caught up in this! Slow down, Nat. This is NOT what I want, and I'll be damned if lose my life to this bastard again!

Natalie's hands slid down further, unzipping his leather pants. "I can't get your pants off any more than I can get mine off with my ankles cuffed," she breathlessly cajoled. Lost in primal lust, Jared reached around and unlocked the ankle cuffs.

"I've got him!" Natalie prevailed, knowing she could easily outsmart a man lost to his urges.

Natalie lulled him into believing she was a willing participant, knowing she would outwit him and escape.

Role play continued as she gave a surreptitious smile and jerked at the waist on his pants, encouraging him to slide off her and allow for their removal. Once on his back, Natalie hovered her sumptuous body above his, holding her arms rigid on either side of his sculpted torso, her hips tantalizing and close beside him on the bed. Her long hair hung like a silk curtain around his chiseled face as she teased him with her tongue.

Jared moaned and reached up, pulled her hair and bit her slender neck. Natalie gasped in surprise when he extracted blood and sucked at it as if he were a vampire. She clawed down his brawny chest, drawing blood to divert the painful bite. His teeth released their hold, and she pulled away as blood dripped down her throat and between her breasts.

Jared grabbed her arm and pulled her hand to his mouth, licking his blood from her fingers. Natalie gave a throaty laugh, as if enjoying the moment. She pulled her hand away and teased her fingers down his chest to his unzipped pants and began vigorously stroking him. As he screamed out in ecstasy, Jared closed his eyes in anticipation. Natalie caught the element of surprise by using the hilt of the sword, still laying on the bed, to bash against his temple, rendering him unconscious.

Natalie fervently searched Jared's pockets for the key to the handcuffs. Safely in her possession, she secured his wrists and ankles to the bed, using the handcuffs he had put on her. Having been imprisoned by them herself, she was confident he would not escape. A flannel shirt from his closet adequately covered her as she waited at the foot of the bed for him to awaken. He will know this ended on MY terms, she declared to the Universe. I stand here victorious, representing every woman who has been tortured, abused, and oppressed.

Groaning with pain, Jared attempted to reach for his head, only to discover his hand encumbered. Thrashing, he bellowed with fury, realizing he had been betrayed.

Natalie took the sword and forced the tip against his carotid artery, pressing enough to draw blood. Jared stilled, comprehending the perilous situation. A crazed persona possessed his demeanor.

"Do it! Impale me! I want to feel the euphoria!" Jared demanded.

"I should kill you," Natalie taunted, with a faraway gleam in her eyes.

End this on your terms, not his, a voice cautioned, snapping Natalie out of her trance.

Using the edge, she sliced the sword against his cheek, mimicking the injury from their past lives. "You don't get to die on your terms!" She viciously spat, throwing the sword to the ground.

"Don't you fucking leave!" Jared roared as she

turned and walked away, knowing the camera caught it all. He thrashed against the handcuffs hard enough, Natalie feared he might break free. To her satisfaction, they held tight while Jared fought, looking like a man possessed.

Lisa's custom ringtone sounded on a phone as Natalie wandered into Jared's kitchen. Numbly, she walked to the device and recognized Lisa's artwork made into a phone case, cradling Lisa's phone.

"Oh my God!" Natalie exclaimed. "Why does Jared have her phone? Has he been the one texting me, pretending to be Lisa or has she been in on his plan to abduct me?"

Natalie's mind attempted to further rationalize, but was so traumatized, she could barely think clearly. Instead, of dialing 911, she picked up Lisa's phone and called Andrew.

Chapter 19

The front door blew open, startling the begeezes out of Natalie. Who was it?

There stood a crazed man on a mission. Andrew's wild eyes darted methodically, assessing surroundings and advancing in a military tactical maneuver with his handgun drawn. The phone call from Natalie assured him she was alive and where to locate her, but until he saw things for himself, Andrew assumed the worst.

"Natalie!" he called out, and only heard a moan. Dear God, he thought, if something happened to my sister, I will be beat the crap out of him!

Natalie's eyes were filled with shock as he approached the barstool in Jared's kitchen. Slumped over slightly, lifting her head, Andrew noticed she was in a catatonic state, just starring ahead as if through him. "Nat," he whispered as he carefully approached her, lowering his weapon so as not to jar her into a deeper state of fear. Her eyes brimmed with unshed tears and her brother was fuming inside, wondering what transpired.

Slowly, she turned her head and met his gaze. "Jared? I mean, Andrew, is that you?" looking at the fear and concern on her little brother's face. Extending her hand out, "Andrew," she sullenly called out his name, still in a stupor. She could sense his concern and reassuring presence, which served as a catalyst for her to release the turmoil in her own mind and relax for a moment. Gasping for breath, her beautiful face sullen, her brother rushed to hold her. Overwhelmed with emotional chaos, she leaned over and slipped safely into his arms, whimpering, screaming, and practically losing unconsciousness in her agony. Her body laid limp against her brother, while he cried his own tears of compassion and relief at the site of his overwrought sister.

Andrew's eyes grew enormous with anger when he heard metal clanking coming from the bedroom down the hall. He did not know what he was facing. His veins bulging in his jaw, his eyes beet red, and the idea of Natalie's abuser in the next room made him furious.

"Natalie! I own you! You are mine for all eternity! This is not the end!" The rants echoed from down the hall, forcing Natalie to become more responsive.

Andrew accompanied his sister over to the couch so he could evaluate the situation. He noticed the bleeding bite wound on her neck and shuttered with despair . He popped his knuckles and strode down the hall.

"Stop!" Natalie demand, as her brother was heading straight towards the bedroom. He turned his head with a vengeance, with a look of murder in his eyes.

"I have to ask him something only he knows," she demanded. "Please let me go speak to him."

"You are not going near him!" Andrew seethed, unwilling to let his sister expose herself to further trauma.

"This is my karmic battle. I've already won, but I have to tie up one loose end." Natalie's tone was not to be trifled with, despite her battered appearance.

Andrew followed her as she stumbled into the bedroom, hovering nearby with his pistol drawn. His mouth hung open to discover what his sister had managed to achieve.

"Stop here." She held her hand up to indicate he should walk no further and pointed to the camera. "We're being recorded," she whispered.

Her brother nodded in understanding, still in awe of her capabilities, speculating what the hell took place here in this chamber.

Natalie summoned her strength to face her abuser again. With shoulders squared and chin erect, Natalie did her best to exude the power she realized she now acquired over Jared. She stood on the side of the bed where the camera stood. She wanted to be certain she would be heard as it recorded.

"Did you kill Lisa?" Her heart felt as if it were in a vice, dreading the answer, even though in her heart, she thought she already knew.

"You were loyal to her instead of to me!" Jared taunted, maliciously smiling.

"Did you kill her?!" Natalie screamed with venomous force.

"Release me and I'll tell you!" he baited, thrashing at the handcuffs and shaking his legs to be released.

"The police can release you after they've taken humiliating pictures of the deranged sex maniac who got himself handcuffed to a bed!" Natalie mocked. "This is where we end. Forever."

Turning, she shut off the camera and picked the sword up from the floor. Andrew had never seen his sister so determined, so full of fury and ready to do what she had to at any cost. He wanted to stop her, to intervene, but his inner voice kept him still. He wanted to protect her.

"I'll be holding this as a reminder. No one has a right to torture me ever again." Wiping Jared's blood from the sword across the leg of his leather pants, she eyed it again. Memories of her past life nightmares flooded her mind. She envisioned how many times Jared had used a sword to kill those she loved, including herself. A yearning gnawed at her need for vengeance.

"Natalie…" Andrew cautioned, sensing his sister's temporary moral weakness.

Her eyes slowly raised to meet her brother's, revealing a hardened hatred.

"Killing him would keep you from being able to fulfill your Soul Contract to help more victims, remember?"

Andrew's words snapped her mind back to the reality of the action she was contemplating.

Natalie drew a full breath and relaxed her grip on the sword. He was right. My desire to counsel the abused and battered is my mission. Especially now that I know how daunting it is, personally. Instead, she leaned over Jared and spit in his face. "You met your match. I'm done," she taunted before exiting the room, leaving him clamoring after her. Tuning out his pathetic cries, she left that world behind her.

"I have to admit," Andrew confessed, following her back to the kitchen, "I was going in there for retribution. That guy was going to get beat within an inch of his life… but you took care of it!"

Natalie rested the sword on the kitchen bar top and stepped away, looking as though she were still contemplating using it. Every nightmare flashed before her eyes, reminding her of how deep this karmic debt went. Making resolve was the only way to empower oneself.

Andrew sensed her emotional struggle and added, "I still want to kill him, but watching you almost take his life brought that impulse down a notch. He's not worth spending the rest of our lives in prison. At least there's video proof of what he's done, and he will spend the rest of his life as a prison boy toy."

Natalie regarded her brother with reluctant agreement. "There's a lot on that video. It mortifies me to think Police Detectives will judge what I had to do to survive. Andrew, I had to play his game."

Realizing his sister would be on the first part of the video as a captive, rage surged through her brother. He knew he couldn't kill Jared, but he would not let the son of a bitch get away without a taste of his own medicine.

"Wait here," he sternly commanded, giving his sister a warning look.

"What are you going to do?" Natalie panicked.

"I won't kill him," Andrew called over his shoulder as he entered the bedroom chamber.

Natalie heard the door lock followed by a repeated cracking of the whip. Eying her new sword, she contemplated joining her brother. It's tempting, but that's not who you are, Nat. She could hear Lisa's voice say in her head. Let it be; don't create more Karma with him.

Gosh, it's like Lisa is right here in my head. How can I hear her? Are we living in two worlds?

Eyes closed, Natalie nodded. I know. I'm so glad I can still hear your voice, she telepathically responded before slumping to the floor, physically and emotionally exhausted. Lisa, I need to find you!

Just like Monet, I'll always be with you. A subtle whisper crossed her thoughts, a calmness overcame her and deep inside she knew, yes, Lisa would always be there.

Blood spattered Andrew's clothes as he emerged and returned to Natalie. He found his sister curled in a fetal position on the floor, spent from her ordeal. He looked like he had just returned from a military battle. Worn out, courageous and defending those he protected.

"Oh my God, what did you do!?" She brought herself to a seated position, assessing his appearance.

"I gave him a taste of his own medicine. And I took this." He held up the video camera. I need to know your reputation is protected. We'll put it in a safe deposit box in case you ever need it. By the way, I had a chat with Jared about coming near you again." Andrew wagged the camera in the air. "This is leverage and blackmail. We can call the police, if you want."

Natalie hoisted herself into the corner of Jared's austere, modern couch. "I'll let fate decide what happens to him. Great idea to use the videotape as blackmail."

"Fair enough. You sit tight while I erase all traces we were ever here. When I got your call, I had a feeling I was going to need to erase evidence. Trust me, I am extremely qualified to make it all disappear."

Natalie's brows arched in surprise before she settled down on the couch and rested her head.

After Andrew was finished, he found his sister dozing, embracing her sword. He scooped her up, the weapon firmly clutched by the hilt in one hand, and carried her to his car. Opening the passenger door, he noticed a white feather resting on the seat. "How did that get there?" He muttered. "Nat, the weirdest things happen when I'm around you."

Natalie smiled to herself, knowing it was a sign from above she was being watched over. "We should call the police," she reluctantly suggested. A vague figure of a male, an older man, flashed before her as, as if the 'angel' was showing his face, finally.

"We'll let him sit for a while before calling someone." Andrew calmly stated on the drive to their mother's house. "There's no rush."

Upon arrival, Natalie went straight to the room, exhausted. I hope I don't dream tonight; she whispered to her angel.

Chapter 20

"You ready for a new adventure?" Andrew was as enthusiastic as a schoolboy at recess to deliver his news the next morning.

"Only if Monet can come!" Natalie seriously answered. "We're a team, you realize?" She winked and smiled, placing her hand on Monet's head and scratching her sizable ears.

"Well, yeah! Monet is a perfect sidekick for this!"

"What's my new adventure?"

"You were fast tracked to be the Lead Psychologist with my unit!"

Eyes wide with astonishment and excitement, Natalie squealed in awe. "This has got to be a sign from the Universe to do something different! I've been giving it a lot of thought in case I got the position."

"You're going to accept it, right?!" Andrew asked, with an implied expectation in his tone.

Natalie grinned and saluted her younger brother, "Yes, little bro!" She crumpled up a napkin and playfully threw it at hm. "New scenery will lend me the chance to heal and get away from so many reminders until I come back."

Andrew fist-pumped a display of his approval. "Remember, it's only supposed to be for six months."

"That's perfect, actually. I have learned so much recently. It has been quite the experience of standing in my own power. I proudly did not allow myself to be the subject of someone's control. Until Ed Bowden and Jared appeared, I didn't know there was a need for me to access my strength. Honestly, I didn't really know what it was. Understanding my past life experiences and the generational patterns they repeated will help me put an end to the suffering. I have a new skill set to draw from to support other women! However, I need a little time to heal myself before I can effectively help someone else. Six months is terrific."

Their mother emerged from the kitchen, wiping her hands on a dish towel. Her long salt and pepper hair had been twisted up in a clip, one wisp hanging in her eyes. "So, you'll be returning? I wasn't certain if you had given it any consideration. I hate for you to go, but I realize a change will do you good."

"I agree. I have a few loose ends to tie up first, mother. I suppose nothing happens by coincidence, so I know taking this job for a while is the right thing to do. I love North Carolina, though, and Asheville is central to where my support system has always been. Running away solves nothing."

Louise sat on the couch across from her daughter, curious about future plans. "Natalie, I feel extremely grateful we could bring the past to light. Will you return to your job when you get back?"

"Mom, so much has brought peace to me finally. Thank you for revealing the truth. I was confused not knowing my own faith structure for years. I needed to understand so much. Looking back, I realize dad's fear, his judgement and how it made you anxious was a huge misunderstanding of my perception. Ben helped me understand my gifts, how to use them and what being an empath entails. I now realize, I've always been using these gifts to help my patients, as well. I'm no longer ashamed and this feels so empowering. As for my work, trauma and PTSD are my specialty, and I can personally relate. Something exciting is happening and I want you to be the first to hear. I plan on starting up my Healing Center specifically for women."

Andrew sat his coffee down and glanced at his sister with admiration. "You're fewer than twenty-four hours away from escaping a second abduction and you've already developed a plan to heal other women? Damn, sis, you're making me look bad!"

Their mother used the dish towel to dab tears of relief and pride. She bowed her head with a humble smile. A sense of deep resolve poured into her heart. No longer did she require to feel guilt or regret.

Natalie blushed, not keen on receiving praise. "I had come up with the concept after my first 'encounter' but this last one gave me new experiences I know women need help to recover from. It gave me the idea to make a variety of healing modalities available. I'm going to ask Ben if he will consider offering past life regressions, soul retrievals, and teach others how to trust their intuition. I can help counsel them through their revelations. It will be a complete healing package."

Goose bumps appeared on Natalie, her brother, and her mother. They all stared at each other with intrigue as they inspected their arms and legs. Andrew blurted out, "Is it only me, but do any of you notice a presence here with us?" They all nodded.

"Well, there's your sign!" Andrew declared.

"There is one more element I need to include. Something mom said helped me to realize there are people like me who are gifted. They must be able to understand and develop those gifts instead of being forced to feel evil! I grew up kneeling by the bed begging for forgiveness for the way God created me! Now I am grateful God provided me with a gift to support people. I do not feel cursed any longer."

"I'm so sorry," her mother offered an apology with a catch in her voice. "I wish I had the wisdom and courage to stand up to your father. I feel partially responsible for what has happened to you. If you had the freedom as a child to develop your intuition and skills, imagine what could have been different…"

Natalie shook her head vehemently and held her palm up for her mother to stop. "I'm sorry, mom, I wasn't blaming you. This is undoubtedly an area I need to mend. I absolutely believe everything takes place as it should in its own time frame. Yes, I resented the hell out of dad for a long time. I forgive him now. I HAD to go through these experiences so I can be effective at helping other women. That was the lesson his soul agreed to help me learn in this lifetime. He was fulfilling his role."

Louise's face lit up with comprehension and she

smiled, relieved. "You are definitely a wise woman and I feel honored to be your mother."

"Mom, imagine the classes I will teach about the truth of spirituality; unconditional love, oneness, and acceptance. Coercive fear tactics will intimidate no one into believing things the man made religion teaches. They called our ancestors uncivilized, slaughtered, and forced them to convert their beliefs in the name of religion. I intend to offer validation and retribution for their suffering." Natalie stopped herself and took a deep breath.

"I could go on for days about this and we could have an amazing discussion, but I digress from what I was saying. The center I want to develop has the capacity to can be educational and healing. I know it will make a tremendous impact in this community."

"I think that's a wonderful plan! Does that mean I get to keep Sage for a while?" Louise asked, intentionally inserting humor as the plump feline rubbed against her shins. Mom always had a way of avoiding deep issues and wanting things to be fun and perfect.

A pang of sadness touched Natalie's emotionally bruised heart at the thought of leaving behind her cherished kitty. "We'll see what my new schedule looks like. Seven hours is too far to drive from Cherry Point to drop her off when I accompany missions."

"Speaking of which, we've got to nail down details for you!" Andrew redirected the conversation.

"When do I start?"

"Two weeks! Not much time, but enough to give notice to your current job. The military will pack and move your things or place them in storage. You can crash at my place until you find one. You will start with the unit on a mission."

Natalie stood up and stared out the large window at the trees gently swaying in the breeze. Sage jumped up on the sill, her tail twitching at a squirrel. Natalie stroked the cat's luxurious fur while attempting to process the rapid changes she faced. "I guess you stay here for now," she choked out. "I'll miss you terribly, but six months will fly by!"

"The thought of a big change scares me, but the thought of trying to return to life as usual frightens me more. My life will never be the same. I know I'll be helping people, but the idea of what it entails is intimidating. There's no handbook on how to be a Dream Warrior."

"Thank God for Ben to guide you with that." Her mother offered for comfort and patted her on the shoulder. A gentle reminder passed through Natalie's thoughts "Ben always patted me in every lifetime to reassure and comfort me."

Natalie nodded in agreement. "I've got a lot to do if I start in two weeks. I've got to get going!" She shook off her sadness and refocused. "I'm going to start by going to work and my apartment office."

Andrew stood up. "I'll walk out with you. There are a few things I need to take care of," he said, giving his sister a cryptic look. He put his hand up to his ear, as if to make a phone call. Natalie nodded and understood his message.

Their mother kept quiet, observing the non-verbal communication between those two. She knew something was up, but let them have their privacy. After all, I kept secrets for years; they could have a few.

Outside, Natalie was frantic as she nervously looked around. "What do we do about Jared?! Have you called the police or anybody?"

"No, that's what I need to take care of. I can't call from my phone or they will trace it. I have to get a disposable one."

"He's been chained up all night!" Natalie almost screamed, worried.

Andrew held a finger to her mouth, shushing her. "How long do you think he left his other victims like that?" her brother retorted, unconcerned. "I deal with assholes like this for a living. Let me take care of it."

"What happens if they find out we were there? Mom knows it's a secret, but no one else can know! I can't go to jail, Andrew." Natalie had kept her panic well hidden, but was close to losing her mind from overthinking.

Andrew gently cupped his sister's face and softened his voice, aware she was still traumatized. "Do you trust me?"

"Completely." She met his earnest gaze as he took one of his hands and gently smoothed her forehead, wrinkled with worry.

"Then when you get in that shiny new car of yours, leave all of this here. I've got it. Jared ends NOW. Okay?"

Natalie's body visibly decompressed as she let go of her concern. They stood in the driveway holding each other until Natalie regained her fortitude.

"Thank you," she humbly expressed.

Andrew responded by giving her an affectionate kiss on the forehead and a gentle slug on the arm. "You're my hero, sis. You really do have superpowers. Call me if you need a masked bandit today."

Natalie smiled and walked to her car, regaining her Wonder Woman strength.

The new metallic midnight blue 4-Runner was nice, but she missed the familiarity of her old one. She drove along the Blue Ridge Parkway, taking in the lush landscape still green despite the winter. Natalie drove too fast, hugging hairpin curves, daring herself to slow down. Are you trying to kill yourself? an angel whispered in her ear. It wasn't long before she found herself driving towards her apartment. The initial intention was to give notice to the front office she would not be renewing her lease. However, a mysterious pull was drawing her to go inside her apartment itself.

Listen to your intuition, she counseled herself. There's something you need to see. Her ears started ringing as if someone was trying to convey a message. She fought to keep the car from racing through the tiny areas where speed traps lurked on the way to the interstate, eager to solve the mystery. Natalie's curiosity occupied her mind as she ruminated over what could be awaiting at her apartment.

As she arrived at The Town Square and walked from the assigned parking spot in the garage, the old energies of fear and paranoia lingered. Natalie glanced around, wondering who had been watching her; Ed, Jared, or both. Her body instinctively shivered with the memories.

The door opened, she precariously stepped inside. Ghosts filled the surrounding space, their energies lingering. Natalie saw herself sitting in the overstuffed cream chair, Sage in her lap, and a glass of wine on the end table. The laughter from the gang of friends, close since high school, filled the air from their last get together when they learned of Natalie's stalker and came to help. A bittersweet smile graced her face at the memory, and she fought back tears.

I can't believe it's only been a week or two since so much happened here and how much has changed, she reminisced.

Jared's image in the kitchen and dining room broke the spell and turned Natalie's blood cold. Natalie closed her eyes and uttered a prayer, "Thank you for protecting me, helping me to end the Soul Contract with Jared, and to find my life's purpose!" Empowered, she turned and followed the entity, guiding her attention.

An object she hadn't noticed before caught her attention. A pair of sunglasses wedged in the couch cushions beckoned to her. A jolt of energy ran through her body as Natalie touched them, pulling the glasses free. It felt like someone had punched her in the gut upon realizing they were Lisa's. Her hand trembled and breathing became erratic while Natalie fought for control of her emotions.

Put them on, she heard Lisa say.

Shaking hands donned the dark-rimmed spectacles. Instantly, a slide show flashed before Natalie's eyes of herself and Lisa together, beginning at childhood. Images of them playing dress up, building sheet forts in the living room, swinging on the playground, running through the trees, bare feet wading in the lake, driving for the first time, high school dances, and always laughing.

"It has been our best lifetime together!" Lisa's voice lovingly exclaimed.

Natalie smiled through tears, wondering how she had any left to shed.

Don't cry, I'm guiding you! We've got work to do together, Sister, but I have to be on this dimensional plane to help. You've gone through a lot, but it's all part of the plan. Trust me. Remember when we tried astral planing in our dreams? Think of it the same way!

Natalie nostalgically smiled and nodded her head in acknowledgment, brushing away the tears and summoning her newfound strength.

Andrew wasn't kidding! A new adventure awaits! Lisa exclaimed. Natalie shook her head, smiled, and choked out a much needed laugh. A slight sensation of healing spread through her heart and mind, knowing Lisa was fine and was still her funny, loving soul sister.

Trust me the same way you trust Andrew! We've

got this!

"Letting go of my false sense of control will not be easy, but I trust you both!" Natalie responded, ready to begin a newfound way of life.

Before you take the glasses off, I've got a few more things to show you.

Intrigued, Natalie made herself comfy in her favorite overstuffed chair and tucked her sculpted legs up beside her. "I'm glad no one can see me. I look ridiculous sitting alone in my apartment wearing sunglasses and talking to someone who isn't here!"

Lisa responded by revealing an image of herself as a chambermaid. That was not one of my best lifetimes, she joked.

"Nor mine!" Natalie wryly retorted, recalling her lifetime in France.

I was a terrible mother, Lisa admitted as she showed Natalie the image of herself in Malaysia, slapping her daughter across the face.

"You ruined my makeup," Natalie joked.

Ha! Seems to me you did that all by yourself! Well, that dog contributed.

"That dog was Monet, you know!"

Yeah... Monet is yours. She was always supposed

to.

"Why are you showing me all of this?" Natalie asked as an image of a jealous wife in Afghanistan appeared.

I want you to understand I am attempting to learn life lessons, too. I am learning to love myself enough, so I don't feel jealous or threatened by other women. Specifically, you. Your Soul agreed to help me overcome my insecurity. I just want to say thank you and I love you!

"We're not done yet!" Natalie reassured her best friend.

Not by a long shot! Lisa agreed. Gotta run!

"Run where?!" Natalie shouted, full of questions, but Lisa left quickly.

Natalie propped Lisa's sunglasses on top of her head and left, knowing it was time to move forward.

Two weeks flew by in a whirlwind with responsibilities to wrap up. The first was searching for her best friend.

"I can hear you, Lisa," Natalie spoke out loud, "but I don't know where you are, so I have to file a report." No reply came from her absent friend.

The following day, a familiar detective came to take Natalie's missing person report. Handsome, with a sexy sideway smile, she wished they had met under better circumstances.

"Please come in Detective Spencer," she stepped aside to show him into her mother's house.

A spark of attraction electrified the air as he entered. Butterflies in her stomach caught Natalie by surprise when he turned and smiled at her. "You had better call me Luke," he urged as he took her hand to shake it, but held on for a while longer than necessary.

Natalie could sense his mutual attraction, and a thrill of excitement ran through her heart.

"My best friend, Lisa Ingall, has been missing. None of our mutual friends have heard from her nor has her mother, who is flying home from France to help look for her."

"Does she have a boyfriend?" Detective Luke Spencer inquired.

Natalie knew how to control her body language, despite hiding emotion, as she answered. "She was seeing someone named Jared. I met him twice, but I don't even know his last name. The last time I talked to him, he said she had gone to an art show out of town. Lisa never texted me from the art show, although I had reached out to her. That surprised me because I had been in a serious car crash and subsequently kidnapped." Oh, and you'll find her phone on his kitchen counter, she wanted to add.

Luke's eyes snapped up and searched her face to see if she was emotionally okay. With a concerned smile, he asked, "How are you doing following that ordeal?" The Detective had been at the scene in response to Natalie's 911 call from Ed Bowden's house.

A genuine smile graced her beautiful face. "I'm recovering really well, thank you!" she emphasized.

"I'm going to be taking a temporary six-month assignment with my brother's military unit to get away and reset my mind."

Detective Spencer's face fell with disappointment.

"I'm coming back, though, to open up my practice counseling abused women. Perhaps that will give us the opportunity to work together?" Natalie asked hopefully.

"Six months is going to seem like an eternity, but you can count on seeing me again when you get back." Luke flashed his sexy smile, making Natalie feel like a giddy schoolgirl. Hurry up and find Lisa so I can tell her all about you, she pleaded to herself.

Natalie supervised the packing of her apartment contents into storage pods, attended an emotional farewell party from her former coworkers, and fielded follow-up questions from the police. A news report about a man found handcuffed to his bed flooded the media for a few days before fading from attention.

Andrew and Natalie both released a sigh of relief as they drove to the airfield to leave on the mission.

"Did I ever tell you who all the players were in my nightmares?"

"Let me see if I can guess!" Andrew loved a game. "I'm thinking Ben was always the kind man who helped you."

"Yeah," Natalie smiled fondly.

"I'm so glad mom has been learning from him! I'm still awestruck at the changes in her personality and belief system! But, I guess if you consider she's learning her life lessons and changing, it's not a surprise." Natalie reflected, watching the scenery go by. "In between missions, I plan on spending some time with Ben on a weekend to do more healing work."

"Healer, heal thyself." Her brother responded and reached over to give her a supportive squeeze on the shoulder.

"I have talked little about Jared." Andrew's jaw and grip on the steering wheel tightened as Natalie tentatively looked at his profile. "He was my husband in all the nightmares."

"He abused and then killed you in each one." He tersely summarized.

"Except this one! Like you said, Jared ends NOW! Thank you for helping me through this ordeal."

With a wink Andrew responded, "Just filling my role here on Earth, Sis!" He indicated with a nod to look ahead. "We're here! Are you ready for your new adventure?"

Natalie took a cleansing breath. With excited anticipation on her face, she opened the door and answered, "Hell yeah, I'm ready!"

Strapped into a military plane alongside Andrew's unit, Natalie and Monet appraised their new comrades in route to a classified location. She held the feather that was mysteriously waiting in her seat as they boarded the aircraft. Looking up, she asked, "Is this you, dad? Are you watching over me and sending feathers as a sign? Is this your way of saying you are sorry for the pain I dealt with all these years? I think so." A new sense of purpose and freedom gave Natalie hope. A personal history of each member of the unit was her reading material for the long flight.

Andrew perused a newspaper as his sister delved into her new responsibilities. In the Local and State section of the paper, Andrew's eyes stopped at a headline reading, Sex Tapes Found, the article cited as a follow up to a previous report. It stated, a man who was found handcuffed to a bed, has now been arrested following the discovery of multiple sex tape recordings in his home, involving women who are believed to be missing. The phone of a local missing woman was found in his home. Andrew raised his eyebrows, remembering his sister's statement; "I'll let fate decide what happens to him." He raised his eyes to the heavens and gave a salute.

Reading further, Andrew's heart caught in his throat at another headline; Woman's Body Found. The article described an unidentified female's body found in a wooded area on the outskirts of Asheville. No identification has been made. He glanced at his sister and kept the information to himself. Let her move on, he thought.

Engrossed in her new responsibilities Natalie tested her gifts by focusing on each team member. I'll pull up their file and note the information Spirit gives me, she planned. Flashes of details came faster than she could document. This is exhausting, she realized. Using my energy to connect to Spirit drains me! I hope I will build up a tolerance; she reflected, as her eyes grew heavy. Perhaps Ben can teach me how to harness this energy and protect myself, she thought.

In the twilight of the sky, gazing out the window and drifting off to sleep, a thought vaguely entered her consciousness. "As a Dream Warrior, I wonder when I start..."

Piercing screams filled the air as Natalie crouched, hidden in the brush. Men with guns, dressed in uniforms, rode horses through the encampment, slaughtering Indigenous women and children after assaulting them. Teepees lay in ruins and pieces of clay pottery littered the ground. A lone little girl dressed in a buckskin gown teetered nearby, eyes wide and in shock. Natalie darted from her hiding place and snatched the toddler, bringing her to safety. She looked into Natalie's soul with large doe eyes. This dream was one of power and guidance. Gone was the fear she had felt in previous nightmares. Instead, it was replaced with wisdom.

"You are my Dream Warrior." She spoke perfectly, so Natalie could understand. "I have been waiting for you."

Author's Final Notes

I hope you enjoyed this book and continue to follow Natalie on her future journey!

It was my intention to bring awareness to issues through the art form of reading entertainment. One of those issues is the oppression of women throughout time. If you look at the research sources I supplied, you see Malaysia, Afghanistan and the Democratic Republic of the Congo listed.

Initially, I researched the history of women's rights in these areas, and many more. I am outraged to discover they have made few changes towards improving women's rights in many areas of the world, especially the three locations where Natalie's past life memories took place.

Each nightmare, or past life, is based factually upon both past and current conditions in those countries. I am blessed to know laws protect me and my daughters where I live. Unfortunately, generational trauma and behavior patterns still exist and threaten us, including friends who have endured suffering at the hands of abusive men. I hope that by calling attention to this inhumane conduct, we can educate ourselves to demand better and put an end to the cycle. Destructive patterns of behavior have become commonplace and quietly accepted. It is my aspiration we can use our voice and our strength to change the unacceptable and teach a newfound respect for all life.

 The narrative of Natalie and her younger brother, Andrew, despising the dreaded Vacation Bible School and going to church is an authentic account about myself and my younger brother. We are Native American Indian from my mother's side and both resonate with the spiritual beauty of our ancestors. I wanted to highlight their love and respect for the Earth and nature, which brings us lessons and healing. Native American culture teaches a way of life through honor, integrity, and a profound spiritual connection. They do not judge, outcast, kill, persecute, promote fear, or control in the name of The Great Spirit, or God. Native American beliefs and way of existence, to me, is a more civilized society. I am honored to be of Creek descent and to focus attention upon their plight.

Our metaphysical capabilities tie together oppression and spirituality. Natalie eventually embraced her gifts. Woven throughout characters in the book were gifts all of them possessed, as does every person. Each one of us is a Divine being having a human experience. We are not a body; we are a soul, part of a collective. The capacity to connect to the Divine Source of the collective, called God, The Great Spirit, etc. and with each other using those gifts, is innate. God does not make mistakes, so why create us with intuition and extrasensory perception if (S)he did not mean us to use them? I believe we each excel with unique skills to help each other navigate our human reality. Natalie pursued developing her skills with Ben, a Native American Shaman, because I wanted her growth to be in the purest, ego-free form I could imagine.

I have sought enlightenment and had pitfalls with mentors unable to overcome their ego, so I shied away from that manner of personal development in my story. I urge you to expand your horizons of ideology to include the gifts you were born with and seek the truth of spirituality. It is my belief it does not exist in a book or a temple, but in our hearts.

You can find more on my spiritual journey in my short story, *Forces Of Nature*, in the collaborative book, *Awakening The Consciousness of Humanity*.

About Jenny

Jenny Macomber is a collaborative author in the #1 Bestseller Awakening The Consciousness of Humanity. Her story, titled Forces of Nature, chronicles how beginning from birth, nature followed her with signs and lessons. As she learned to connect with nature, she found healing and connection with life that had been waiting to expand her consciousness.

Jenny's newest book, While She Was Dreaming, started off as a short story and quickly evolved into something exciting as she expanded ideas, originally based on a real life experience. This book delves into past lives, psychic gifts, and the reality of what lies beneath the surface in our forgotten past. Twists and turns follow its character, Natalie, as she fights to survive nightmares coming to life!

Jenny is a fun-loving, spirited, strong-willed lover of nature and family. Born and raised in Winter Park, FL, she now resides in in Colorado Springs, CO with her husband, twin daughters, and son-in-law. Jenny loves hiking and exploring the beautiful state of Colorado! She has a connection to the diverse wildlife and nature that surrounds her.

Jenny is a researcher and advocate for wellness and truth. She is currently working on two solo books; one fiction, the other about her daughter's chronic illness so as to help others searching for answers.

A former special needs occupational therapy paraprofessional, Jenny is blessed to work on her books from home now while devoting herself to the needs of her family. As an Intuitive and Reiki Master, she uses her gifts to convey messages while being a conduit for Divine energy. She is passionate about the connection between the mind and body for complete health and alternative healing modalities which address the root of illness. Her ability to channel messages aides in every aspect of her life, including writing!

Her spiritual path has led to continued growth and personal wellness as she has navigated traumatic life events. Jenny strives to help others by sharing her journey and giving hope, love, validation and empathy. It is her hope to be a beacon of light for positive change!

Follow Jenny on her website at JennyMacomber.com, on Facebook at Jenny Macomber, Author, and on Instagram at macomberjenny.

Sources

CSH, Sunny Ray, 'Reincarnation Belief of the North American Indians', 10 June 2021, sunnyray.org/Reincarnation-American-Indians.htm

Vashundhra Gupta, 29 Sept 2018, My Spiritual Shenanigans, 'What are Soul Contracts & How Do They Influence Our Spiritual Journey?', 30 July 2021, myspiritualshenanigans.blog/soul-contracts/

Sam Boomer, Awake and Align, 'What are Soul Contracts and How Do They Work?', 30 July 2021, awakenandalign.com/soul-contracts/

Amnesty International, 25 Nov 2014, 'Women in Afghanistan: the back story', 28 March 2021, amnesty.org.uk/womens-rights-afghanistan-history

Homa Hoodfar, 27 July 2021, The Conversation, 'Taliban 'has not changed'; say women facing subjugation in areas of Afghanistan under its extremist rule', 30 July 2021, https://the conversation.com/Taliban-has-not-changed-say-women-facing-subjugation-in-areas-of-afghanistan-under-its-extremist-rule-164760

Scott Levi, Origins, Sept 2009, 'The Long, Long Struggle for Women's Rights in Afghanistan', 4 March 2021, origins.osu.edu/article/long-long-struggle-women-s-rights-afghanistan

Lauren Bohn, 8 Dec 2018, Time, 'We're All Handcuffed in this Country'. Why Afghanistan Is Still the Worst Place in the World to be a Woman', 4 March 2021, time.com/5472411/Afghanistan-women-justice-war/

Wikipedia, 16 Nov 2020, 'Cherokee Spiritual Beliefs', 28 July 2021, en.wikipedia.org/wiki/Cherokee_Spiritual_beliefs

Shweta Advani, Mind Journal, 'The Native Americans' 7 Core Beliefs About Dreams', 9 July 2021, themindsjournal.com/7-core-native-american-beliefs-about-dreams/2/

Mateo Sol, 12 July 2021, 'Soul Retrieval: 3 Powerful Ways to Heal Soul Loss', 17 July 2021, lonerwolf.com/soul-retrieval/?utm_source=e-mail&utm_medium=social&utm_campaign=socialwolf

Reliefweb, 7 March 2017, 'Women's Rights in Africa', 17 May 2021, relief-web.int/report/world/womens-rights-africa

Wikipedia, 10 July 2021, 'Women in Africa', 17 May 2021, en.wikipedia. org/wiki/women_in_Africa

Judith Wanga, 27 March 2010, The Guardian, 'Why Congo is the world's most dangerous place for women', 17 May 2021, theguardian.com/lifeand-style/2010/mar/28/congo-women-danger-war-judith-wanga

Wikipedia, 11 Aug 2021, 'Sexual Violence in the Democratic Republic of the Congo', 17 May 2021, en.wikipedia.org/wiki/sexual_violence_in_the_Democratic_Republic_of_the_Congo

UN Women Asia and the Pacific, 'Facts and Figures: Ending Violence Against Women and Girls', asiapacific.unwomen.org/en/focus-areas/end-violence-against-women/evaw-facts-and-figures

Wikipedia, 23 July 2021, 'Women in Malaysia', 17 May 2021, en.wikipedia. org/wiki/Women_in_Malaysia

Web Desk, 20 Feb 2015, Tribune, 'Female Circumcision on the rise in Malaysia', 17 May 2021, tribune.com.pk/story/841392/female-circumci-sion-on-the-rise-in-Malaysia

Liz Gooch, 12 Aug 2016, 'Malaysia's Child Brides' Men accused of rape are marrying their alleged victims to avoid prosecution. 17 May 2021, www. aljazeera.com/2016/8/12/malaysias-child-brides

Made in the USA
Las Vegas, NV
13 September 2021